Secret of the Pack Rat's Nest

By Martha E. Rhynes

*To Samuel Luke
Hope you enjoy my book.
Martha E. Rhynes*

Copyright © 2012 by Martha E. Rhynes. All rights reserved. No part of this book may be reproduced in any form or by any electronic or mechanical means, including information storage and retrieval systems, without permission in writing from the author and the publisher, except by a reviewer who may quote brief passages in a review.

Trademarks and advertising slogans used in this book belong to their respective companies.

Illustrations of dog, bicycle, and football are copyrighted by Dover Publications Inc. and used in accord with their guidelines. All rights reserved.

Book design by Stephen B. Bagley.

ISBN 978-1-300-04881-7

Printed in the United States of America

10 9 8 7 6 5 4 3 2 1

To my best critics:
Willard Rhynes, Stephen B. Bagley,
Carson Taylor, & Beth Peterson

To teenage readers who may be inspired to write a book

To the members of Ada Writers

CHAPTER ONE

Colby's low-down feelings stuck to him as tight as a tick on a dog's ear. Oh sure. He'd cheered the Bartlett Bulldogs during the pep rally, and he'd jazzed up the fight song on his trombone, but his heart wasn't really in it. What he wanted more than anything was to play football, but he'd quit the team because he couldn't stay after school to practice. After his dad's accident, he'd taken a part-time job delivering the afternoon and Sunday morning newspapers. The pay was small, but every dime helped a little.

To lift his spirits, Colby stopped at the YMCA and parked his bike in the rack. From the doorway, he could hear the thump, thump, thump of a basketball being dribbled down the court and screeches of rubber soled shoes on the polished gym floor. "Shoot! Shoot!" someone shouted.

Travis Turner, Eddie Imotichey, and two other seniors were on the court playing a game of pick up. Skeeter Wilkins, a skinny black kid, sat on the bleachers watching the action.

"Hey, Skeet, why aren't you in the game?" asked Colby.

Skeeter shrugged. "Travis won't let me play. He says I ain't big enough."

"Then they don't know about your long shot, do they? C'mon. Let's show 'em!"

Travis was hogging the basketball, slowly thumping it down the court when Colby ran up behind him. He reached under Travis's arm, and with a deft motion, stole the ball and passed it to Skeeter, who swished it through the net from center court.

"Great shot!" said Eddie, a tall Chickasaw, whose straight black hair was tied back in a ponytail with a leather thong. "Hey, Trav, we got enough guys to choose up sides. I choose Colby and Skeeter against you three."

"What? Those two punks? Why, we'll whip your butts!"

For thirty minutes, the six boys ran up and down the court, yelling and shooting baskets and rebounding. Eddie, Colby, and Skeeter rolled up a big score, while Travis and his teammates struggled to rebound. If they guarded the basket, Skeeter ripped shots from the outside. If they guarded Skeeter, then Eddie and Colby slipped inside to make easy lay-ups.

Sweaty and red faced, Travis elbowed Colby in the ribs and tried to trip him as they ran side by side down the court. Colby passed the ball to Skeeter, who was crouched near the sideline ready to shoot another three-pointer. Like an angry bull, Travis turned and charged Skeeter, shoving him out of bounds toward the bleachers, where he sprawled on the floor.

"Hey, man. You've got no call to rough me up like that," complained Skeeter. "This here's just a game, you know."

Scowling and breathing hard, Travis jerked Skeeter to his feet by the front of his shirt. "Listen here, you little punk, if you can't take the rough stuff, go home and play with your baby dolls," and he twisted Skeeter's tee-shirt so tightly in his fingers that when he released him, the wrinkles stuck out from his flat chest like tiny breasts. Wide-eyed, Skeeter stepped out of Travis's reach and smoothed the front of his shirt.

Colby grabbed Travis's shoulder and spun him around. "Who do you think you're shoving, Travis? Skeeter may be little, but I'm just your size. Try shoving me!" Colby was as tall as Travis, but the older boy outweighed him by thirty pounds of hard muscle.

"You freshmen don't learn very fast, do you, Elliott?" Travis flexed his shoulders and biceps and slapped his left palm against his right fist. "Mess around with me, buddy boy, and you'll be sorry – very, very sorry," and he started toward Colby.

Suddenly the Y director appeared in the doorway. "All right, you guys. Cut out the rough stuff or out you go. You know the rules."

"I'm gone," said Eddie Imotichey, and without looking back, he and the other boys strolled toward the exit.

Still full of bravado, Travis swaggered after them. He paused in the doorway. "Just watch your step, Colby, or I'll take care of you and that black kid when you least expect it."

Colby wanted to punch Travis in the mouth, hard enough to bloody his lip and knock out a couple of teeth, but instead, he threw the basketball at the hoop with such force that the backboard vibrated.

Skeeter placed a hand on Colby's shoulder. "Thanks for taking up for me, dude," he said. That Travis – he's one mean gorilla."

"Yeah. He's the kind of bully that sneaks up on people and stabs them in the back. You stay out of his way."

Outside, Colby looked around for Travis, but he was gone. Then he strapped his bicycle helmet under his chin and pedaled down Delmonte Drive toward Linda's house. Just seeing her always made him feel better. If her dad's home from work, he thought, I'll give him a complimentary copy of the *Bartlett Banner* and maybe score a few points with the old grouch.

"Bull's eye!" he shouted as the rolled newspaper hurtled through space, slid across the porch and landed kerplop in front of the Jenkins' front door.

A slender girl in blue jeans and a pink tee shirt waved from the doorway. At her signal, Colby jumped the curb on his bike, coasted down the driveway, dismounted, and vaulted gracefully over the porch railing.

Linda Jenkins sat in the porch swing and patted the seat beside her. Her smile, in spite of silver braces on her teeth, made Colby feel like a big-time athlete and movie star. He flopped down on the cushion beside her and set the swing in motion with his foot. As they rocked back and forth, he nervously smoothed his unruly auburn curls with his fingers and felt the downy fuzz of whiskers on his chin. He wanted to hold Linda's hand, but his own hands were black with newsprint. Her smooth skin and lips were pink and shiny, even without makeup, and her long brown hair was still damp from a shower. Colby could smell her cherry-scented shampoo.

He looked into Linda's pale blue eyes, fringed with dark lashes, and remembered how delicious her lips tasted, pressed against his, after he gave her the ring with the blue stone that matched her eyes. He'd won it throwing darts at balloons on the midway at the county fair. The Ferris wheel stopped to let off passengers, and as they sat swinging in a seat at the top, he'd slipped the ring on her finger. The memory of that kiss was still magic.

"Who do you think will be crowned band queen tonight?" Linda said, and she leaned closer to Colby and squeezed his arm.

"Well, if my campaign speeches did any good, you won the election, hands down. Nearly every freshman and sophomore in the band voted for you. Melissa and Pam probably split the votes among the juniors and seniors."

"Oh, Colby, you're such a sweetheart," she gushed. "Do you really think I have a chance?" The direct gaze of her blue eyes into his hazel ones had the stunning effect of an electric current.

Colby stammered, "Well, sure! Seniors don't rule everything, you know."

Linda frowned and tossed her head. "Especially seniors with bad reputations like Melissa and Pam. Everybody at school knows about Melissa Marshall. If she does half the bad things Dalton Barrett says she does, she's absolutely trash."

"Aw, Linda, you shouldn't believe all those rumors. Guys like Dalton make up stories about their ex-girlfriends to impress other guys. I've heard lots of stuff like that in the locker room. Besides, you helped the band win a gold medal at the state music contest. Not many girls can play the trombone. We were real proud of you."

Shrugging her shoulders, Linda gave her damp hair a flip and said, "Well, I did my best. Melissa plays clarinet like a quacking duck, and Pam's just as bad. She drops her baton every time the twirlers perform."

Colby liked Melissa and Pam and refused to believe the gossip about them, so he changed the subject. "Who's going to escort you onto the field tonight?"

Holding her hands in a prayerful pose Linda said, "Would you believe that Dalton Barrett is escorting me? Travis Turner is escorting Melissa, and Eddie Imotichey is escorting Pam. You know the tradition – senior football boys and band girls."

She jumped up from the swing and whirled around on one foot. "Dalton sent me a corsage that looks like a tiny white pompon with blue and gold ribbons." She giggled. "He's coming by for me at seven in his Corvette. Oh, Colby," she sighed. "I'm so excited I could just die!"

Colby gritted his teeth and clenched his fists. He leaned his head against the back of the swing and closed his eyes, trying to smother his jealousy. What chance does a guy like me have with a girl like Linda? He thought. No car, no money. Why should a smart aleck like Dalton get all the breaks?

Linda smiled at his scowling, red face, and lightly walked her fingers up the sleeve of his blue jean jacket. "Don't be jealous, Colby. After all, Dalton is captain of the football team." She patted his shoulder. "I'll sit by you until half-time when the band marches onto the field for the ceremony."

Big deal. The thought of Linda riding in Dalton's black Corvette and standing by him during the homecoming ritual changed Colby's clear hazel eyes to a muddy brown, like creek water after a flood. Unable to control his anger any longer, he rose swiftly, leaped over the porch railing, and mounted his bike.

"See you at the game, Linda," he growled and left her, open-mouthed, standing at the porch railing.

CHAPTER TWO

Pumping hard with slim, muscular legs, Colby pedaled down the street, weaving in and out through five o'clock traffic. Whiffs of hickory smoke mingled with tantalizing aromas of hamburgers and fried chicken. Fast food restaurants lined the busy street. Toward the south end of Delmonte, near the edge of town, traffic dwindled, and crisp autumn air cooled his frustration and anger.

A perfect evening for the Bartlett-Tushka game, he thought. Colby loved sports, especially football, but his paper route interfered with varsity practice after school. Since his dad's accident, he'd delivered the afternoon and Sunday morning editions of the *Bartlett Banner* to help pay for his clothes and school supplies. Tom Elliott had fallen from the second floor balcony of a motel he was remodeling. Because he was self-employed and had considered himself immune to accidents, he had no medical insurance.

A conversation outside his dad's hospital room put an end to Colby's playing football. "We're really short of money," his mother had said. "Your father's medical bills have wiped out most of our savings." She searched in her purse for a tissue to dry her tears. "I've taken a job in the hospital cafeteria so I can be near Tom while he's in rehab, and you must get a job after school to help us meet expenses. As soon as your dad's back heals, he'll be able to work, and then you can go out for sports again."

But Colby knew Tom Elliott's recovery would require a miracle. After a lengthy stay in rehab, he continued to use a wheelchair, but he could take only a few steps to the bathroom with a walker. The accident had certainly changed their lives.

Last year, Tom had won a cross country race, he'd coached a summer league baseball team, but now, bitter and depressed, he either sat in his wheel chair watching television, or slept his pain away on a rented hospital bed. Colby worried about the number of pain pills his father took.

Dr. Perry prescribed back surgery but warned if the surgery was unsuccessful, Tom might become paralyzed. And without insurance, the surgery and rehabilitation would be very expensive. Every night, the Elliott family prayed that Tom's back would miraculously heal itself.

Jeanie Elliott left the house at 4:30 A.M. daily to supervise the cafeteria at Bartlett Community Hospital. Colby fixed breakfast for himself and his father and made his bed. He sometimes washed a load of clothes and packed his lunch before he rode his bike to school. After school, he delivered the *Bartlett Banner* to customers on his route.

Most of the time Colby could talk himself out of downer moods, especially if he stayed real busy. First things first, he rationalized. After all, he was only a freshman. He had three more years to play football for the Bartlett Bulldogs.

At the edge of town, just before Delmonte ran into Highway 10, he wheeled his bicycle into the driveway of the Chickasaw Trading Post, managed by the father of his best friend, Bert Pickens. Built like a two-story log cabin, the store was located at the edge of 320 acres of Chickasaw Indian land, allotted to the Pickens family before Oklahoma became a state. Actually, the trading post was just an ordinary convenience store, but Mr. Pickens also sold fishing and hunting licenses and bought and sold pecans.

Bert was restocking shelves with canned goods and keeping an eye on the gasoline pumps while his parents ate supper in their upstairs apartment. He was student-manager of the Bartlett Bulldog athletic teams. Bert knew how to wrap a sprained ankle and how to stop a nosebleed, and he knew almost as many winning strategies as Coach Blevins.

"Think the Bulldogs will win tonight?" asked Colby.

Bert ran his hand over short black hair and adjusted his glasses. "I hope so, but it won't be a snap. Sure do wish you were on the team, Cole. We need somebody like you to handle the ball. Dalton's got the bighead so bad he can hardly pull his helmet on. He thinks some college recruiter is going to sign him on as quarterback when he graduates. None of the other guys on the team can stand him. My cousin Eddie and I call him "Darling" Dalton behind his back 'cause he thinks he's such hot stuff with the girls. But you watch. When that 250 pound Tushka tackle hits him tonight, he'll fumble."

"Well, I sure hope the Bulldogs win," said Colby. "I'd ten times rather be out there playing on the field with the guys, than sitting on my butt in the stadium with the band."

Bert grinned. "I know just how you feel, Cole. Bench warming ain't no fun! Here, try a stick of this beef jerky. Mom makes it herself," and he pulled a stick out of a glass container on the counter and offered it to Colby, who bit off a piece of the salty dried beef and put the rest in his pocket. He couldn't remember a single time he'd been in the trading post that Bert or Mr. Pickens hadn't given him something – like the jerky, or a stick of candy – to take with him when he left. He guessed it was a Chickasaw tradition to show they were friends.

"Thanks, Bert," he said. "I'll see you tonight at the game."

As he pedaled out of the driveway, he hummed the Bulldogs' fight song. Playing first chair trombone in the band did have a few rewards. Linda played second chair trombone and sat beside him on the bus when the pep band went to out-of-town games. Besides, morning band practice didn't interfere with his paper route.

He had thought about trying out for drum major. He knew he could put more zip into the half-time performance than the current drum major who would graduate in June. But strutting down the field with a baton just wasn't the same as running down the field with a football to score the winning touchdown.

He was late, so he made an abrupt left-hand turn and took a short cut down a narrow alley that bordered the old Weston Estate. Weeds and trash covered ancient red brick paving. Horse-drawn buggies and early model cars had once rolled down the lane. Now, a washed-out culvert prevented cars from using it, but not bicycles and hikers.

Years ago the Weston gardener had mowed the grass and pruned shrubs lining the road, but city workers no longer maintained it. Now people ignored the NO DUMPING sign and tossed garbage into the drainage ditches. Huge cedar trees screened the gloomy mansion from the eyes of anyone who walked down the alley.

Long shadows, cast by limbs and yellowing foliage of pecan trees, formed a tunnel through which Colby passed. The lane had been a favorite parking spot for lovers until someone started the rumor of hearing a werewolf's howl when the moon was full. Colby remembered sitting around a campfire with Skeeter and Bert last summer and listening to Skeeter tell a scary story about a witch who lived in the creepy old mansion.

Dismounting from his bike, Colby kicked some beer cans from the littered road and walked beside his bicycle. Heavy undergrowth of flaming red sumac and persimmon sprouts partially concealed a spiked iron fence. Walking slowly, he stooped to pick up a few of the fallen pecans that littered the path and stuffed them into his jacket pocket for a later snack.

As Colby approached a massive wrought iron gate, framed by pillars of white native limestone, a huge black dog loped down the driveway, barking furiously. With his head and neck extended, and his lips curled in an angry snarl, the dog lunged at the iron bars. His bared white fangs looked sharp enough to tear flesh from bone. His ears lay flat against his skull, and short hairs on his back bristled like needles. Afraid that with one more lunge, the black dog would be out on the road, ready to kill, Colby leaped back.

He placed his bicycle as a shield between himself and the snarling dog who thrust his muzzle through the bars of the fence and snapped at the tires and spokes. Careful not to make eye contact with him, Colby eased past the gate, keeping up a steady stream of assurances. "It's okay, old buddy. See. I won't hurt you."

Then he remembered the strip of beef jerky in his pocket. "Here, boy!" He threw the jerky at the feet of the angry dog. To Colby's astonishment, the dog stopped barking, wolfed it down, and stood at attention with his head up and ears cocked.

Colby continued pushing his bike past the gate and down the lane. As he mounted his bicycle, his legs felt like limp rubber bands. When he dared look back, the black dog was sitting quietly behind the gate, alert, and on guard.

CHAPTER THREE

Colby remembered the scary story Skeeter had told Bert and him about Miss Weston and her black dog. Back in August, the boys had set up camp on the banks of Turkey Creek, a clear stream that bubbled up from a huge aquifer beneath the earth's surface and flowed into the Red River.

Colby and Skeeter had cleaned and filleted a nice mess of bass they caught while Bert, who always acted as cook on campouts, put together a dish he called cowboy potatoes. He carefully peeled and sliced potatoes and onions and tossed them into a deep kettle that had a thin layer of hot bacon grease in the bottom. Then he added a large can of tomatoes and salt and pepper and placed a lid on the pan and set it aside near the campfire to steam.

"Hurry up, man, I'm starving," said Skeeter, as he smeared peanut butter on a slice of bread and crammed it into his mouth to ease his hunger pangs. Colby popped the lid of a root beer and downed it in one long gulp. Then he burped loudly.

They watched with hungry eyes and growling bellies as Bert rolled the bass fillets in yellow cornmeal and salt before dropping them into a skillet, where they sizzled and crackled in hot fat. As darkness fell, the boys sat beside the dying campfire and pigged out on crispy pieces of fish and cowboy potatoes piled high on paper plates.

Then, with glowing embers lighting their faces, Colby and Bert told scary stories – about Norman Bates and the movie *Psycho,* and Stephen King's *Cujo,* and that new *Twilight* film about vampires and werewolves.

Skeeter said, "Okay, guys. It's my turn, and I'm gonna tell you a real story. It ain't made-up like the ones you told. It's about that old lady who lives in the haunted house on Weston Hill." He took a deep breath. "Folks around town claim she's a vampire."

He lowered his voice. The only sounds were cicadas buzzing and the crackle and pop of the fire. "They say she murdered her sister and her father, but they couldn't prove it. Their bodies are buried in a graveyard behind the house." He took a deep breath and gazed upward toward the full moon, now visible above the tree tops.

"When the moon is full," Skeeter whispered, "Old Lady Weston lures young lovers who park on the road to come inside her creepy old house. Then she hypnotizes 'em and ties 'em up and drinks their blood. After that, they turn into vampires and sleep in coffins in her basement."

"Dang, Skeeter," said Colby, breaking the spell. "How could that little old woman tie up a kid like me? Why, I'd just give her a judo chop and run."

"Maybe so," Skeeter said. "But vampires have magical powers, you know, and anyhow, if any of her victims try to escape, she sics her black werewolf on 'em."

Bert laughed. "That's bull, Skeeter. I've seen her in our store buying dog food. Miss Weston is an old hag, for sure, but a vampire? No way!"

"Okay, okay. But remember what I done told you and don't never park and make out with a girl on Weston Hill, or you'll be sorry." At the thought of Skeeter and a girl parked on Weston Hill or anywhere else, Colby and Bert roared with laughter.

As the boys lay on their backs looking at the stars, Colby recalled seeing Miss Weston crossing the street while he and his folks waited for the light to change on Delmonte, just a few days before his Dad's accident. Walking with the aid of a cane, she shuffled across the street in front of their pickup truck.

Even in the August heat, she wore a long black coat and a man's felt hat, tied with a black scarf so that the brim concealed her face. On her feet she wore a pair of high topped black canvas tennis shoes. To Colby, she looked like the wicked witch in *The Wizard of Oz*. He wondered why she didn't just hop on her cane and fly, instead of hobbling across the street.

Tom had remarked, "You'd never know it by looking at that old woman, Colby, but she's probably the richest person in this town. She walks downtown once a month to consult her lawyer and banker and buy a few groceries."

His mother said, "Why, she's nothing but a bag of bones. I wonder what she eats."

"Probably little kids," Tom said and chuckled.

"Don't be silly," Jeanie said. "I feel sorry for her. She looks so frail and helpless."

"There are lots of rumors about the Weston family," said Tom. "The story goes that Old Man Weston was a rich widower with two daughters. He made his money on land speculation about the time Oklahoma became a state in 1907. Then he hit it big during the oil boom in the thirties.

"The girls lived a life of luxury. They traveled in Europe, went to boarding school in Switzerland, fancy clothes, servants, you name it. They came home about the same time Hitler invaded Poland. Neither of the daughters ever married – too good (or too ugly) for the men around here, I guess.

"Anyhow, one day the old man and one of the girls died mysteriously. They're buried in the family cemetery right there on the estate, but gossip has it Miss Weston done 'em in! No charges were ever brought against her, but folks think she's the Lizzie Borden of Bartlett."

"Who's Lizzie Borden?" Colby asked.

"A woman who lived in Massachusetts back in the 1800s. She was accused of murdering her father and stepmother with an ax," said Jeanie. "Lizzie was acquitted because the evidence was circumstantial, but to this day, people continue to wonder whether or not she did it. I don't see how anybody could get away with a heinous crime like that in Bartlett."

"Don't be too sure of that, Jeanie. After the Weston funerals, that old bag of bones, as you call her, fired all of the servants, and she has lived by herself for nearly sixty years. Mighty suspicious, I'd say."

Tom lowered his voice to a whisper and gave Jeanie his Count Dracula vampire leer. "Bleah, bleah," he said, rolling his tongue. "Folks say those who enter the iron gates to Weston mansion never return." Jeanie smiled and gave Tom a shove in the ribs with her elbow.

The light at the intersection changed. Tom shifted gears and resumed his normal tone of voice. "Too bad the place has such a bad reputation. I think Weston Hill would be the ideal location for patio homes. And I'm just the guy to build them."

Colby remembered that day with sadness. Dad never told stories or cracked jokes any more. Even though Dr. Perry bragged about how much Tom had improved, Colby knew his dad suffered much pain by the way he gritted his teeth when he moved from his wheelchair to the bed.

   Colby pedaled up the driveway and parked his bike in the carport. He entered the kitchen and called, "I'm home." Tom and Jeanie were in the den watching the evening news on television, so he made himself two peanut butter sandwiches with mustard and dill pickle slices, poured a large glass of milk, and strolled into the living room. They smiled in welcome but continued to concentrate on the news program. Still wearing her cafeteria uniform, Jeanie sat beside Tom and held his hand.

   Since Mr. Davis, the band director, required band members to be at the stadium early, Colby quickly ate his sandwiches, showered, shaved his sparse mustache and chin whiskers, and applied after-shave lotion. After examining his face in the bathroom mirror, he dabbed some medicine on a pimple and slathered deodorant under his arms. Then he tucked a long-sleeved knit shirt into his jeans and stepped into his band uniform. Two layers of clothing added padding to his slender frame. He buttoned his blue jacket and adjusted a loop of gold braid that hung from his shoulder.

   Then he put gel on his cowlick and combed his wavy auburn hair. He checked his appearance in the full length mirror on the closet door. Not bad, he thought, but what will Linda think?

   "Well, I'm off to the game," Colby said to his parents, as he shoved his wallet containing an ID and two dollars into his pocket. "See you about midnight." With one hand on the doorknob, he paused.

   "Who's playing tonight, son?" asked Tom.

   "Bartlett Bulldogs against the Tushka Tigers. It'll be a great game. Tune in to KBAR. We're having the king and queen homecoming coronation at half-time and a victory dance after the game in the gym."

   "Victory dance, huh? Then the Bulldogs better win."

   "Be careful coming home, Colby, and be sure to take your heavy jacket and a warm cap. The weatherman predicts a cold front."

   "Okay, Mom."

   "Do you still have reflectors on the front and back of your bike?"

   "Sure thing. Gosh, Mom. I'm not a baby."

   "Well, I worry about you riding your bicycle in traffic, especially late at night."

   "Where's your trombone, son? How will you get it home?"

   "No problem," said Colby. "Mr. Davis always brings our instruments to the football stadium in the van, so I don't have to bother with it before or after the game. I'll hang my uniform up in the van."

"Need any money?" asked Tom.

"Naw," replied Colby. "I'll get into the game free, and the dance just costs a dollar. I've got plenty," he said and patted his hip pocket. Then jamming his blue shako with the gold plume on his head, he pedaled his bicycle toward the football stadium, Home of the Bartlett Bulldogs.

CHAPTER FOUR

High intensity stadium lights illuminated the field and the parking lot behind the high school. As Colby chained his bicycle to the fence surrounding the stadium, tantalizing aromas of buttered popcorn, coffee, hot dogs, and onions made his stomach rumble, but he needed money to get into the dance and a dollar for two cokes – one for himself and one for Linda, so he ignored the tempting smells.

Band members began arriving in their blue and gold uniforms, all but Linda, Melissa, and Pam, who wore fancy gowns beneath their band jackets. Linda blew little puffs of frosty vapor as she struggled to climb the stadium steps with her mum corsage in a plastic container in one hand and her trombone case in the other. Colby hurried to assist her. They seated themselves in the band section and began to assemble their horns and tune up with the other brass players.

"I am so nervous and my mouth is so dry I can't even blow into my mouthpiece," complained Linda. "I don't know if I can walk onto that field in front of all of these people during half time. Just look over there. Melissa isn't even a bit nervous."

"You'll be fine. You look great, Linda. Just remember. The band will be standing behind you during the coronation."

Soon the stadium was filled to capacity. Fans from Tushka filled the grandstand on the visitor's side. Football players from both teams warmed up on the field, running sprints, passing and catching the ball, and kicking field goals. On the sidelines, Bert Pickens arranged the first aid kit, towels, water jugs, extra jerseys, pads, and other paraphernalia at the end of the home team bench. He waved to Colby.

Enviously Colby watched his former teammates running up and down the field in their pads and blue jerseys. Coach Blevins had not yet awarded Number 22 jersey to anyone else, which gave Colby hope that he might wear it again someday.

As he watched the players on the field, Number 28, Dalton Barrett, kicked a perfect field goal. Then he turned toward the bleachers, where Linda was sitting in the band section, and gave her a thumbs up sign. Colby gritted his teeth as she stood and waved back to Dalton. Soon both teams retired to the dressing rooms for pre-game pep talks.

Out on the track that encircled the field, cheerleaders in blue pleated skirts and gold sweaters led fans in stunts and yells until the crowd reached a high pitch of excitement.

Beat 'em, Beat 'em,
Bartlett High.
V-I-C-T-O-R-Y!
Can we win it?
Well, I guess!
Bartlett Bulldogs,
YES! YES! YES!

Cheerleaders formed two lines in front of the dressing room, and two girls held up a large hoop, covered with butcher paper with Beat 'em Bulldogs painted on it.

Mr. Davis raised his baton, Skeeter gave a drum roll, and the band played the Bartlett High School fight song. Dalton Barrett, followed by his teammates, burst through the paper-covered hoop and ran onto the field. The fans cheered wildly.

Dalton and the Tushka captain faced each other for the toss up, which Dalton won. He chose to receive the ball. Both teams stood silently with bowed heads as Principal Pembroke gave a brief invocation over the loud speaker, and the band played the national anthem, followed by the school song. Then Skeeter gave another drum roll as the Tushka fullback kicked off.

Dalton ran past Eddie and another teammate in the backfield and called for the catch with upraised arms and fingers in a V-for-victory signal. To the Bartlett fans' dismay, he fumbled the catch on the ten yard line, and the Tushka Tigers scored a touchdown in the first minutes of the game. Colby remembered Bert's prediction earlier – about Dalton's fumbles.

At half-time Tushka led 14-7. As the last football player left the gridiron for the dressing rooms, the Bulldog band marched onto the field and formed a semi-circle facing the Bartlett grandstand.

The loudspeaker squeaked and squawked until someone adjusted the sound system. Then Principal Pembroke announced, "Students, parents, alumni, and friends, it is my pleasure at this homecoming game, to introduce our school's royalty. These young women were elected by popular vote of the Bartlett High School band. They are escorted by senior members of the Bulldog football team. And now – the moment you've all been waiting for. May I present Princess Melissa Marshall, escorted by graduating senior Travis Turner."

The band played "A Pretty Girl Is Like a Melody," and Melissa, tall and slender in a gold satin dress, walked slowly onto the field. Travis slouched along beside her. His football uniform was fresh and unstained because he had been sitting on the bench. Fans in the stadium applauded politely as Travis presented Melissa with an arm bouquet of white chrysanthemums tied with gold and blue ribbons.

"Next, may I present Princess Pamela Edwards, escorted by senior linebacker Eddie Imotichey."

Pamela, also in gold satin, and Eddie, clumsy and self-conscious in the glare of the stadium lights, walked slowly onto the field. Skeeter thumped the bass drum in three-four time as the band played "You Light Up My Life." Embarrassed, Eddie examined the toes of his football shoes and shyly handed Pamela her bouquet.

"And now, may I present the Bartlett High School homecoming queen: Miss Linda Jenkins, escorted by senior football captain Dalton Barrett."

Colby's trombone led the band in a jazzy version of "It Had To Be You" as Linda and Dalton stepped forward. Her blue brocade dress with its full skirt accentuated her petite size as she stood beside the tall, handsome football player. Bartlett fans whistled and applauded.

Dalton placed a crown sparkling with gold sequins upon Linda's head. Then, like a scene from a romantic movie, he cupped her chin in his hand, and kissed her with such a long and passionate kiss that Skeeter began pounding time on the bass drum while the crowd cheered and whistled. One-two-three-four-five-six-seven-eight-nine-ten!

When Dalton released Linda, her crown dangled from one ear, and petals were falling from her crushed corsage. Smiling and waving to approving fans, Dalton placed his hand under Linda's elbow and guided her from the field. Melissa, Travis, Pam, and Eddie followed. When Linda, flustered and pink-cheeked, returned to her seat in the stands, band members teased her about the kiss.

Colby tried to pretend it had never happened.

During the final quarter, the Tushka Tigers were in the lead, 14-13. Both teams struggled, back and forth between the thirty yard line markers as they exchanged possession of the ball. Dalton, as quarterback, seldom called plays that featured other backfield players. He tried running up the middle but could not penetrate the stone wall of the Tigers' defense. Then he attempted a fifty yard pass, dancing around in the backfield, looking for a receiver.

Just as Bert had predicted, the big Tushka tackle sacked him, and Dalton fumbled. Imotichey recovered the fumble, and Coach Blevins benched Dalton. Colby felt sure that "Darling" Dalton faked a limp as he moved toward the sidelines and waved to applauding Bulldog fans.

In support of the second string quarterback, the Bulldogs rallied and moved the ball by a series of short passes to the Tigers' fifteen yard line. Coach Blevins paced the sidelines. On fourth down, with seconds left to play, he sent Dalton back into the game. Dalton's field goal in the final seconds boosted the Bulldogs to a 17-14 win.

Without saying goodbye to Colby, Linda rushed onto the field with other fans to follow the triumphant team to the dressing room where she waited outside with cheerleaders and other girls whose dates for the dance were football players.

Colby packed Linda's and his own trombone into their cases and helped Mr. Davis load the band instruments into the van. He removed his band uniform and hat and hung them up, too. Then he rode his bicycle over to the high school gym, where the victory dance was in progress. He sighed as he chained his bike to a rack at the side of the building. His was the only bicycle there.

At the door he paid a dollar to Mrs. McPherson, his English teacher, who always chaperoned school dances, and entered the dimly lit gym. It was decorated with blue and gold crepe paper streamers and balloons. He sat on the bleachers and watched the entrance for Linda and Dalton's arrival. In spite of everything, he refused to believe that Dalton Barrett had won Linda's heart with that Hollywood kiss.

Soon King Dalton and Queen Linda arrived. Everyone stopped dancing to applaud them. Holding hands, the dancers formed a circle around the royal couple and shouted the victory yell.

Skeeter, who was serving as deejay for the evening, put on a fast number, and the dancers spun off, gyrating wildly. Colby watched the bobbing heads of his classmates as they danced alone and in groups, their arms waving and bodies swaying.

Soon Skeeter played a slow number, and Colby threaded his way among the dancers toward Linda. She smiled as he approached, but just as he took her in his arms and began dancing toward the edge of the crowd where there was more room, he felt a heavy hand on his shoulder.

"Get your own date, kid," said Dalton, and he whirled Linda into a tight embrace. He turned his broad back on Colby and maneuvered her to the center of the gym.

Colby could not see Linda's face, but she made no apparent protest. Feeling as if his heart had been ripped from his chest, he started toward the exit. Suddenly, a tall, slender girl linked her arm with his.

"Getting dumped makes you feel like dirt, doesn't it?" said Melissa. "C'mon. Let's dance." And she put her arm around Colby's neck and followed his lead as they slow danced around the floor. His mom had taught him several intricate dips and turns that Melissa followed smoothly until the music ended.

"Colby, you're a great dancer!" she said.

"Thanks. So are you. How about a soda, Melissa?"

"Sure. Why not?"

Sitting on the top row of the bleachers, they sipped their drinks in silence and watched the dancers. Soon Travis came to claim his date.

"Robbing the cradle, huh, Mel?" said Travis with a sneer.

"Hey, you left me on the dance floor," Melissa said. "Anyhow, Colby's a better dancer than you are."

"Well, I'm back, now, so hit the road, kid," said Travis as he pulled Melissa onto the crowded floor.

Colby walked outside the warm gym. He shivered as he buttoned his windbreaker and pulled a cap and gloves out of a pocket. The gym cast dark shadows over the gravel path that led to the bicycle rack.

"Oh, no!" he groaned, as he bent to unlock the chain around his bicycle. Someone had slashed his tires. Shocked by the senseless vandalism, Colby felt as if he'd been punched in the belly. He knelt to examine the damage, and his eyes focused on a small, metal object lying on the gravel. Whoever had slashed his tires had dropped a roach clip that marijuana smokers use. Colby picked it up and shoved it into his jacket pocket.

As he pushed his bicycle home, he kept asking himself who would pull such a mean trick? Only one person came to mind. Travis. At the Y, he'd threatened to get even. But with only a roach clip for evidence,

Colby could never prove it. Every pothead at school has one, he thought.

Without tires, he'd have no transportation, and without transportation, he couldn't throw his paper route, and without his job, he'd have no money. Maybe Mr. Kennedy, editor of the paper, would advance him enough cash for new tires. Tomorrow he'd ask him. He walked home fast to avoid the approaching storm.

CHAPTER FIVE

On Saturday morning, Colby thrust his arms into the sleeves of his denim jacket, and two paper shell pecans fell out of the pockets. He cracked one against the other in his palm and picked out the nut meats. As he chewed the rich, brown tidbits, he remembered seeing hundreds of pecans on the lane that bordered the Weston Estate. For years nobody had bothered to harvest that pecan orchard, and Mr. Pickens bought and sold unshelled pecans by the pound. Well, maybe money does grow on trees – pecan trees, he thought.

After breakfast he told his dad, "I'm headed downtown. I've made sandwiches for lunch, and I left yours in the fridge. I'll be back late this afternoon. Do you need anything before I go?"

"Just hand me a couple of my pain pills, son. I had a bad night – couldn't sleep – so I'll probably try to rest until your mother comes home. Maybe you'd better leave her a note so she'll know where to reach you."

"Just tell her to call Pickens' store. Bert will know where to find me."

Before going to the newspaper office, Colby stopped off at Barney's Bicycle Shop to get a price on tires for his trail bike. Two of the cheapest tires cost $20, and two heavy duty tires cost $40. A sign behind the counter said Cash Only.

"Would you consider charging those tires to me if I promise to pay you next week?" Colby asked.

"Sorry, kid. I've been played for a sucker too many times by teenagers who promise to pay," said Barney. "I've got to eat, too. Come back when you've got the money. I close at six."

At the *Bartlett Banner*, Mr. Kennedy was sympathetic, but he didn't offer to lend Colby money for the tires. He said, "That's a shame, Colby. Sounds to me like some coward did it. They damage property of people they envy; sometimes people they don't even know. Can't your folks drive you around your paper route until you get the bike fixed?"

"No sir. My dad's not able to drive because of his back injury, and my mom works at the hospital."

"Well, I'll help you Sunday morning, but you'll need to get your own transportation by Monday. If you don't, I'll have to assign your route to someone else. Let's see." He looked at his calendar. "I'll come by your house about six after I've distributed the Sunday edition to the other carriers. Then I'll drive you around your route in the truck. Be ready at six. I'll honk."

Colby shouldered his backpack and walked down Delmonte to Pickens' Chickasaw Trading Post. Behind the store was the pasture, where Bert kept his horse Toni, and behind that was Turkey Creek, where the boys fished. Across the road was the Weston Estate.

Mr. Pickens sold cigarettes and gasoline and picnic supplies. In fall, hunters bought licenses and weighed their deer on his scale. In summer, Bert sold minnows and night crawlers to fishermen. Bert's parents were small-boned, brown-skinned Chickasaws with round faces and brown eyes that could look right into the heart of a person. According to Bert, Mr. Pickens was a Vietnam War veteran who had been decorated with a Silver Star and a Purple Heart, but Bert said he never talked about his wartime experiences.

Mrs. Pickens stayed in the second floor apartment and seldom worked in the store. Colby loved to eat supper with them, especially when Mrs. Pickens served pashofa, a dish made from dried hominy and pork sausage. Just thinking about her fried apricot pies made his stomach growl.

As Colby approached the trading post, he saw Bert sweeping the driveway, which was covered with fallen leaves. "Hey there, Cole. Where's your bike?" asked Bert.

"Some scumbag slashed my tires last night during the dance at the gym."

"Gosh. Who hates your guts enough to do something like that?"

"Nobody. Well, now, I take that back. There is one guy, but I couldn't prove he did it. Anyhow, I've got to come up with some cash to replace my tires."

Colby walked around to the side of the store where Mr. Pickens and his nephew Eddie Imotichey were weighing burlap sacks of

pecans and loading them from the dock into the bed of a pickup truck. A sign on the wall read:
    WE BUY PECANS
    NATIVES-$.60 PER POUND
    PAPER SHELLS-$.75 PER POUND

Colby said, "Hey, Eddie, you guys played a great game last night. Way to go!"

Eddie smiled and set a heavy burlap bag on the scale. He adjusted the strap of his oversized, faded denim overalls before he said, "Thanks. We just got lucky, I guess." Then he turned and re-entered the shed for another sack of pecans.

Colby turned to Mr. Pickens. "If I gather some pecans, would you buy them from me?"

"Sure. But where do you aim to find them, son?"

"Lots of pecans have fallen from trees that overhang Weston Lane, and I don't see how anybody could claim they own the ones lying on the road."

"You're right. Nobody harvests them. Most folks won't go near the place. But a word of warning, Colby, just be careful and don't climb the fence or trespass on the estate. Miss Weston has a mean guard dog."

Mr. Pickens paused to help Eddie replace a torn sack. "I'll buy all the pecans you bring in, but you'll need some sacks." He pointed to a bench. "Take a couple of those burlap bags."

Bert stopped sweeping leaves and said, "Gosh, Cole, you mean you're gonna pick up pecans on Weston Hill? What about the werewolf and the vampire? Aren't you afraid?" Bert rolled his eyes and pretended to shiver.

"Heck, no! Not when I need money! Besides, it's Saturday afternoon and broad daylight. Werewolves and vampires don't come out until dark. Why don't you come with me and stand guard?"

"Can I go with Colby, Dad?" Bert asked. "I've swept off the driveway."

"If you'll be back about two. Eddie's taking this load of pecans to the warehouse, so I'll need you to watch the store while I'm busy with folks who want to buy and sell pecans." Mr. Pickens zipped up a quilted hunter's vest over his rumpled khaki work clothes. "Before you go, boys, make yourselves some sandwiches and take a couple of sodas out of the box. Just remember: Do not trespass on the Weston Estate. Stay on the road."

Inside the store, Bert slathered mustard on four pieces of bread. From the meat counter, he removed a stick of bologna, cut slices half an inch thick and made two tube steak sandwiches, which he wrapped in butcher paper and placed inside a brown paper sack. He added a root beer, a strawberry pop and two candy bars. Then he smiled and picked up a long fork. "How about a Kosher dill pickle with garlic? Garlic is supposed to keep vampires away."

"Sounds good to me," said Colby and he watched Bert stab two green cucumbers floating in a gallon jug of brine. Then before he closed the paper sack, Bert opened a jar of beef jerky and tossed two sticks into the sack.

By midmorning Colby and Bert were on their hands and knees picking up large native pecans on the brick road bordering the Weston Estate. While they worked, Colby filled Bert in on the victory dance, and told him how Dalton had cut him out of dancing with Linda, and how he'd found the roach clip beside his bicycle. He pulled the clip out of his pocket and showed it to Bert.

"Whoever slashed your tires was probably smoking pot outside the gym, and your bike just happened to be there."

"If I ever find out who did it, they'll be sorry. And that's not all. I'm fed up with Dalton Barrett trying to steal my girl. Those seniors think they rule the school. I'll sure be glad when they graduate."

Bert said, "Dalton doesn't have the right to rule anything. Last night in the locker room after the game, Coach really chewed him out over the way he played. Coach said he'd better get in shape and cut out the booze and any other bad habits he has, or he wouldn't recommend him to college recruiters." Bert stood up and stretched. "I sure wish you could play for the Bulldogs, Cole. You run a lot faster than Dalton, and you'd really improve our passing game."

"Not this season, Bert, but as soon as Dad's back heals, I'll be back on the team, for sure."

To hide his doubts about ever playing football again, Colby changed the subject and told Bert about Miss Weston's black guard dog. "He's a cross between a Labrador and a Doberman. Big and strong. Not a werewolf, but I'd hate to meet him on a moonlit night."

"If he shows up, I'm outa here," said Bert.

"Don't worry. He's inside the fence. Anyhow, I know a secret about that dog."

"What's that?"

"He's a sucker for beef jerky."

Hundreds of pecans were hidden in nests of tall dried weeds that grew in ditches bordering the lane. By noon they had filled half a burlap bag. Hoisting it over his shoulder, Bert said, "This must weigh at least fifty pounds. It's all I can carry without a wheelbarrow."

They ate lunch with their backs propped against the spiked iron fence. "You won't believe it," Bert said sheepishly, "but I've never walked this far down Weston Lane before. Scared to, I guess. Brush is so thick along here you can't see much, but I'll bet there's some good squirrel hunting in the trees beyond that fence. Must be a zillion nuts, too. Nobody ever picks 'em up, so you might as well have them, Cole."

"I'd be trespassing, Bert. You know what your dad said about that. I guess I could go up to the house and ask permission to gather the old woman's pecans on the halves, but I don't want to tangle with her or her dog."

With sore knees and scratched hands, Colby and Bert gathered pecans from clumps of leaves and dead grass. They moved from the fence at their backs toward the outer perimeter of each tree's canopy, where pecans had fallen from limbs overhanging the road.

When he came upon a large brush pile in a ditch, Bert said, "Say, Cole, do you suppose those sticks and leaves could hide a pack rat's nest? Dad says pack rats store nuts under tree roots and in brush piles like this. If it's a nest, we can gather ten pounds real fast."

Quickly the boys scattered twigs and brush. Sure enough, from a hollow place beneath a fallen tree limb, handfuls of pecans rolled out. Bert and Colby scooped them up.

"What a windfall!" said Bert. "That old pack rat gave you a head start. You're just plain lucky! If you can put fifty pounds of nuts in that other sack this afternoon, you'll probably have enough money for two tires. Maybe a head start on a new bike."

Bert stood up and stretched. "I hate to run, Cole, but it's time I was getting back, so I'm leaving it with you. I'll tote this sack of pecans to the store and weigh them for you. Come by around dark, and we'll build a campfire and celebrate Halloween in the pasture behind the store. Mom says I'm too old to trick-or-treat."

"Okay. I'll see you this evening. Thanks for helping me, Bert."

A pale sun shone through the bare limbs of the trees and warmed Colby's back. Occasionally the silence was broken by cawing crows and squirrels swishing up tree trunks and out on limbs as they gathered nuts for their winter caches.

Without Bert's help, Colby filled the second sack more slowly. He hoped that after Mr. Pickens paid him for the pecans, he would still have time to get to the bicycle shop before six when it closed. He scraped aside leaves and twigs so he wouldn't miss any pecans hidden in nests of weeds along the road. Now and then he lifted the sack to test its weight. Late in the afternoon as the sun began to set, the temperature dropped. In the distance he could hear a dog barking. As the barking came closer, Colby felt in his pocket for the piece of beef jerky he'd saved from his lunch.

Suddenly the black dog bounded to the spiked wrought iron fence and stuck his head through the bars. Colby could see the dog's strong teeth as he barked a furious warning. His ears were laid back, and his neck and head reminded Colby of a snake, ready to strike.

Trying not to show fear, Colby said, "Well, now, boy, as you can see, I'm not trespassing on your side of the fence." He kept his head down and did not make eye contact with the angry dog. "Just a few more pecans, and I'll have enough cash for my tires. So how about a little treat?" He slowly pulled the jerky from his pocket and threw a piece of it to the agitated dog, who caught it, mid-air. He quit barking but continued to pace back and forth on his side of the fence.

Hoping to calm the dog with friendly conversation, Colby said, "Today is my lucky day, so I'm going to call you Lucky. My name's Colby." He tossed the dog another bite of jerky. The black dog stopped pacing nervously and sat on his haunches, watching Colby as he scooped pecans into the sack.

Sunset had turned to shades of purple and orange when Colby finally filled the second sack to a level that he hoped would weigh fifty pounds. He lifted the heavy bag and started toward Pickens' Store. He walked on one side of the fence while Lucky, growling warnings, guarded the other side. At the gated entrance to the estate, the dog stopped and listened, as if he heard someone calling him from the house. Colby heard nothing.

"So long, Lucky," he said, and he watched the black dog run up the driveway toward the mansion, hidden from view by a dense foliage of cedar trees.

CHAPTER SIX

That evening, Colby, Skeeter, and Bert set up camp in the pasture behind Pickens' store. For a while they took turns riding bareback around the pasture on Toni, Bert's gentle paint mare. Bert had set up two barrels, weighted with sand, about fifty feet apart, so they could race around them on a figure eight path. Bert was an expert at barrel racing – he'd won prizes at local rodeos – but even though Colby and Skeeter gripped Toni's sides tightly with their legs and feet, and clutched her mane, they sailed off her back on the turns. She'd nicker and wait patiently while they dusted themselves off and climbed on again.

Finally Bert said, "You guys will never become rodeo performers, that's for sure. Clowns, maybe, but barrel racers? No way!" He rubbed Toni's back and legs with a tow sack and removed her bridle. Then he gave her an extra ration of oats.

The boys threw lariat loops at a saw horse to which Bert had nailed a bull's skull, bleached white by the sun. Then they practiced rope tricks. Bert could twirl a loop big enough to jump through. "I learned this trick by watching an old black and white film of Will Rogers doing his stuff," Bert explained.

At sundown they built a fire and roasted wieners and toasted marshmallows. Skeeter played cowboy songs on his guitar, and Bert and Colby sang along. The fire crackled and spit sparks into the sky when Bert tossed on another log.

"Dang!" said Colby, looking at his watch. "It's only eight o'clock. This is sure a heckuva way to spend Halloween."

"Halloween just ain't fun without scarin' somebody," said Skeeter.

"Yeah, but we're too old to trick or treat," said Bert.

"We could go to the carnival at the grade school," said Colby, "but that's mostly for little kids who want to show off their costumes."

"Yeah, you'd scare 'em without even wearing a mask," said Skeeter.

"Oh yeah? They'd think you're the Creature from the Black Lagoon."

"Okay, smart guy. But my face ain't half as ugly as yours."

Colby crossed his eyes and made a grotesque face and laughed. Then he said, "The Kiwanis Club has set up a haunted house in the old train depot, but it'll be just more of the same old stuff. You know: Fake spider webs, grape eyeballs, spaghetti intestines, and Mr. Pembroke lying in a coffin with his face painted green. Besides, it costs a buck to get in, and I haven't got any money. I spent most of what I got from selling the pecans on new bicycle tires, and I gave the rest to my Mom."

"Then that cuts us out of going to the midnight show, too. It's a double feature – some old vampire movie: *Bride of Dracula* and *Son of Frankenstein*. I've seen both of 'em."

"Well, heck. Can't we think of anything excitin' to do besides settin' around this campfire like those old geezers down at the Spit and Whittle Club?" said Skeeter.

"Hey, I've got a great idea!" said Bert. "Let's go over to Weston Hill and trick or treat old lady Weston. That would really test our Halloween spirit."

"What if that old woman turns out to be a real vampire?" said Skeeter. "And what about her werewolf dog?"

"Grow up, Skeet! That stuff's just make believe." Bert removed a twig from his mouth and threw it on the fire.

"Whoa, now. Just a dang minute!" said Colby. "I'm not so sure a Halloween prank on Miss Weston is a good idea. Her guard dog's not about to let anybody through those gates. I should know! I've seen his teeth! And remember what your dad said about us trespassing on the Weston property?"

"Oh, that was because of the old lady's pecans. We aren't going to steal her pecans or anything else. We'll just knock on her door and run. Dad won't care. And I've got a great idea about how to get around that dog." He lowered his voice as if an eavesdropper might be listening. "We'll make a lot of noise at the front gate and wait to see if the dog shows up. If he doesn't come running, we'll climb over the fence. I'll bet the old woman shuts him up in the house at night."

"If she does, we can sneak up, bang on the front door, and run back to the gate before she can get downstairs to let him out," said Colby.

"We'll have to run awful fast," said Skeeter.

"Yeah," said Colby. "He's her guard dog. Take my word for it."

"You know what?" said Bert. "Dad's got a can of pepper spray under the counter in the store. He keeps it in case of a robbery. I can get it, and if the dog takes after us, I'll spray him in the face with it. That'll stop him long enough for us to get back to the gate."

"I'd hate to think we'd hurt him some way," said Colby. "He's a nice dog, just doing the job he's trained to do. Wouldn't that pepper spray hurt him?"

"Naw. My cousin Franklin's a cop, and he uses it to control rowdy prisoners all the time."

While Skeeter and Colby packed the food away and banked the fire, Bert went to get the pepper spray. Colby rubbed some of the ashes on his pale skin as camouflage.

Without telling the Pickens where they were going, the boys crossed Delmonte and headed for Weston Hill. The moon shone brightly on the weedy brick path that paralleled spiked bars of the fence. Stone gargoyles adorned the massive gate posts and stared with evil eyes at the Halloween intruders.

Colby tested the latch of the wrought iron gate. It swung open with a loud screech. "If the black dog is running loose on the grounds, that noise will sure alert him."

The three pranksters froze momentarily to listen for the dog's fierce barks and pounding feet. Silence.

"He must be shut up, or else he's takin' a snooze and don't know we're here," whispered Skeeter.

Suddenly Bert howled like a wolf. "That ought to get a response if the Weston werewolf is really on the prowl." Then he howled again. Nothing.

"Okay, guys. It's safe to move up to the house. Stick together. If the dog chases us, Bert can stop him with the pepper spray."

With stealthy steps, they crept up the brick-paved driveway lined with cedar trees, so dense they formed a dark tunnel. The strong, dusty, evergreen scent made Skeeter's eyes water. Suddenly, he sneezed. "Achoo!"

"Shh!" hissed Bert.

"Can't help it. Allergies," whispered Skeeter.

"Shut up," warned Colby. "We're almost to the house."

They emerged from the cedar-lined tunnel and stood as still as statues in front of the three-storied limestone mansion. Silence.

Moonlight revealed overgrown shrubbery and dead weeds in neglected flower beds in front of the verandah.

Like soldiers approaching an enemy camp, the boys crept up the steps and crossed the porch. A huge brass knocker in the shape of a lion's head was mounted in the center of a sturdy oak door. Beveled glass windows outlined the doorway, but the boys could not see what lay beyond the door because the interior of the mansion was dark as a tomb.

Suddenly Skeeter sneezed, not once, but repeatedly. "Ah-choo! Ah-choo! Ah-choo!"

From somewhere inside the house, the dog began to bark, and a light shone from a front window on the second floor. Colby grabbed the door knocker and banged it loudly three times.

"Trick or treat! Trick or treat!" the boys shouted.

Miss Weston raised the upstairs window and screeched in a high-pitched voice that sounded like a witch's cackle, "You poachers think I don't know what you've been up to in my pecan orchard? Trespassing, that's what. Well, I may be old but I'm not blind! Insane asylum's where you boys belong. Planting all those weeds and then pulling them up! I've got a gun, and I aim to protect my property. Now git before I fill you full of holes."

"Run!" Colby shouted.

As they leaped from the verandah and headed for the driveway, Bert turned his ankle and fell. The pepper spray can rolled into the weeds. Limping, he followed Colby and Skeeter across the lawn.

"Hurry!" shouted Colby.

"Can't," said Bert. "I've sprained my ankle."

Suspending Bert between them, Colby and Skeeter ran an awkward, five-legged race toward the cedar-lined driveway.

A shot from a double barreled shotgun sprayed pellets over their heads, and Miss Weston shouted, "Now get off my property and stay off, or next time I'll shoot to kill." Then she released the dog. "Sic 'em, boy," she said.

The distance to the front gate seemed like miles, but fear was a motive for speed. Over the sounds of their pounding feet and labored breathing, the boys could hear the black dog barking as he narrowed the distance between them. Just as they reached the front gate, he caught them. Snarling, the dog seized Bert's back pocket in his razor sharp teeth and ripped off the seat of his jeans. Colby and Skeeter dragged Bert through the gate and slammed it shut.

The dog rammed his head through the bars and continued to bark. Foamy white saliva dripped from his mouth. Taut muscles looked as if they might propel him through the gate.

"Where's that can of pepper spray? That'll shut him up," shouted Skeeter.

"Dropped it," said Bert, panting.

Turning to the angry, snarling dog, Colby shouted. "Shut up, Lucky!" He pointed toward the house. "Home, boy! Go home!"

With his ears cocked, the agitated dog suddenly stopped barking. He cocked his head and looked at Colby as if he recognized the command.

Again Colby said, "Go home, Lucky." The dog turned abruptly and ran toward the house and disappeared behind the cedar trees.

"What kind of voodoo was that?" asked Skeeter, his eyes opened wide in amazement.

"I just guessed the right command. Lucky's a trained guard dog. He must have recognized my command. We're safe now, so let's make tracks. Can you walk, Bert?" said Colby.

"You'll have to help me. That dog's ruined my new jeans, but at least he didn't sink his fangs into my butt."

As the boys stumbled down the road toward Pickens' store, Skeeter said, "What did that old woman mean about us being up to something in her pecan orchard and pulling up weeds?"

"No telling what she meant. Bert and I picked up pecans on the road, but that's on city property. She's probably just paranoid and doesn't like being tricked on Halloween."

Bert said, "Well, it looks to me like we're the ones that got tricked. Heck, we're lucky we got out of that alive. If she'd aimed that gun a foot lower, she'd have filled us full of lead. And how am I gonna explain these torn jeans and sprained ankle to Mom and Dad? I'll be grounded, for sure."

CHAPTER SEVEN

At dawn on Sunday morning, Colby met Mr. Kennedy at the Banner distribution dock. As they inserted copies of the newspaper into plastic sleeves, Mr. Kennedy said, "Since I'm helping you this morning, Colby, would you mind helping me deliver another carrier's route? By working together, we can get the job done twice as fast, and today I'm in a hurry."

"Why, sure." Colby was surprised at how fast Mr. Kennedy could roll papers.

"Ben Mason didn't show up this morning. Officer Reed tells me he was arrested last night for a traffic violation, and they found marijuana and other drug paraphernalia under the seat of his car. He won't work for me again, you can be sure."

Colby and Ben had folded the Banner together many times on this same dock. Ben had dropped out of school before graduation last year. "High school is boring," he'd complained. Most afternoons he seemed okay, but occasionally, on Sunday mornings, Ben's eyes were bloodshot and his clothes reeked of the sweet-sour smell of marijuana.

"Ordinarily, I wouldn't mind filling in for a carrier," said Mr. Kennedy, "but Mary's singing a solo at St. Luke's this morning, and I don't want to miss it."

"Mary? You mean Mary Kennedy who's a freshman?"

Mr. Kennedy laughed. "Yes, Mary Kennedy is my daughter."

Until that moment, Colby had never connected the chubby redhead who sat behind him in English class with Mr. Kennedy, his boss.

"You wouldn't be interested in taking over Ben's paper route permanently, would you, Colby? Somebody's got to do it."

"Well, sure. I need the money."

Mr. Kennedy drove Colby around the two paper routes in his pickup. When he stopped in front of the Elliott's house, he said,

"Thanks for doing double duty, Colby. Now get those new bicycle tires mounted, and I'll count on you to be on the job Monday afternoon."

After breakfast, Colby helped his father dress for church. Attending services and being with friends was good medicine for him. Tom took two pain pills, and Colby pushed his wheelchair up a ramp and into the back of the pickup. Then he set the chair's brake. Sunshine knocked the chill off the November day, but winter was coming, and soon Tom wouldn't be able to ride to church in the truck. We need a van, Colby thought. He wrapped a lap robe around his father's knees and sat in the bed of the truck while Jeanie drove slowly to the church.

During worship service Colby saw Linda sitting across the aisle with her mom and dad, but she did not look his way. She did not sing the hymns and kept her head bowed while Pastor Ingram preached his sermon. Colby wondered what was wrong.

After lunch he mounted and aired up the new bicycle tires he'd bought just minutes before Barney's Bicycle Shop closed on Saturday. His mom and dad were engrossed in a football game on television, so he decided to ride over to see Linda.

Mr. Jenkins answered the door and scowled at Colby, who smiled and said, "Good afternoon, sir. Please accept this Sunday edition of the *Bartlett Banner* with my compliments."

Mr. Jenkins yawned and reached for the paper. Colby had awakened him from an afternoon nap. "Linda's not here, kid. She's gone across town with her mother to visit friends." He yawned again. "Thanks for the paper, but you needn't bother to come back. After what happened Friday night, Linda's not going anywhere for a while. She's grounded. So if you want to talk to Linda, you can see her at school or church. No phone calls, either." With that announcement, Mr. Jenkins closed the door.

Colby stood on the porch for a moment before he grasped the significance of Mr. Jenkins' words. Wow! Linda's old man must really be mad over "Darling" Dalton's Hollywood kiss at the football game. Well, that kiss made me mad too, he thought. Maybe Dalton tried something more than a kiss after the dance.

Feeling restless, Colby left Linda's house and wheeled his bike toward Pickens' Trading Post. He needed to talk, and Bert was a good listener. A sign on the door said, "Gone to Burr Oak Springs. Open 6 A.M. Monday."

It was still early enough to gather a few more pecans, so Colby parked his bike behind the store and chained it to the fence. Then he picked up a burlap bag from the bench and headed toward Weston Hill.

The sun was warm on his back. Except for the faint smell of wood smoke and frisky movements of a few squirrels and birds, there was no sign of life behind the spiked iron fence that surrounded the Weston Estate.

The Halloween adventure made Colby think that Miss Weston was just a paranoid old woman with a guard dog. He didn't intend to climb the fence and trespass on her land, and he didn't need to ask her permission to gather pecans on the road. He knelt at the spot where he had stopped working on Saturday and began scooping up brown nuts by the handfuls. An hour passed. As he worked, Colby thought about his mom and dad and their unpaid bills and how he wished he could earn enough money to buy a van and pay for Tom's back surgery.

Then his thoughts turned to Linda. What a fool he'd been to think she'd ever be his girl. She was so pretty, so popular. If Mr. Jenkins would let her, she could date any boy at school. Compared to cars and dances and movies that other boys like Dalton could give her, the cheap, blue glass ring was nothing. It had turned her finger green.

Lost in thought, Colby did not notice Lucky's stealthy approach. When he turned to explore another tuft of weeds near the fence, he was startled to see the big black dog, his coat shiny as patent leather, sitting on his haunches by a tree trunk watching him. The dog's sharp, pointed ears were raised like two antennae.

"Why, hello, boy. You're mighty sneaky. Sorry, but I didn't bring you any treats today."

Lucky stood with muscles tensed, as if he could not decide whether Colby was friend or foe. Then he cautiously moved toward the fence and sat on his haunches again with his head raised and his ears pointed forward.

"Looks to me like you're one lonesome pup. I'll bet that old woman up there in the house doesn't know you're down here making friends with me. If she did, she'd get rid of you as her guard dog." After a while, Lucky lay down on his side of the fence and watched Colby with his head between his paws.

Colby had gathered only a third of a sack of nuts when he spied what looked like another pack rat's nest. What luck! Some busy little rodent had neatly piled sticks and dead leaves against a fallen tree limb, hoping to conceal a winter's cache of pecans.

Colby quickly shoved the sticks and leaves aside, but instead of a cache of nuts, the brush pile concealed a large, black plastic garbage bag. Now why would anyone hide garbage? he wondered. Usually people who dumped trash on Weston Road just tossed it into the ditches.

Suddenly, as though the dog heard a sound inaudible to Colby, he pricked up his ears and ran off through the underbrush toward the mansion.

Colby unfastened the plastic tab on the garbage bag and looked inside. It contained a lot of pint-sized plastic bags full of dried, green leaves. The substance resembled oregano, an herb that his mother used when she made spaghetti sauce. He carefully opened one of the small, sealed bags. One sniff confirmed his suspicion: marijuana!

Now Colby understood what Miss Weston meant about "trespassers up to something in my pecan orchard." Maybe these hidden bags of marijuana belonged to Ben Mason, the paper carrier Mr. Kennedy had fired.

Shocked by his discovery, Colby sat down. Then he instinctively looked around to see if anyone was watching him. The trees seemed to have eyes. All was silent except for a few sparrows in flight. With his thumb and forefinger, he carefully re-sealed the small plastic bag of marijuana leaves and shoved it into his jacket pocket. Then he counted forty-nine additional bags and replaced them inside the large black bag. He twisted the fastener and stuffed it back under the pecan log.

First he covered the bag with leaves; then he carefully piled twigs on the leaves to hold them in place, exactly as he'd found them. As a final marker, he draped a piece of string from his pocket over the log. If anyone else opened the cache, they'd disturb the string. Whoever had hidden the marijuana stash on Weston Road would never suspect he'd found it.

With thoughts racing inside his head like relay runners on a track, Colby walked back to Pickens' store with the sack of pecans. What should he do with the small plastic bag in his pocket? Should he sell it? He sure could use the money. He knew lots of kids at school who would buy it and keep quiet. Should he report the drug cache to Mr. Pembroke at school or to the police? Would they believe he'd found it by accident? Probably not. They'd ask him lots of questions, and the kids at school would shun him for being a "nark." Maybe he could spy on whoever had hidden the black bag and collect a reward.

In the past, Colby had wanted no part of the drug scene. He thought potheads like Ben Mason or the goon who had slashed his tires were fools. But they had suddenly become a source of money that he badly needed. As he walked, he reasoned that if potheads chose to smoke marijuana and their brains went up in smoke, it was no responsibility of his. And after he sold the first packet, he could come back for the rest of it. It was worth plenty of money – maybe enough to pay for some of Dad's medical expenses. Make the down payment on a van. Selling it wouldn't mean he'd become a user himself. Yeah, but what about Dad and Mom? Or even Mr. Kennedy, his boss. They'd want to know where he got the money. They'd keep after him until he told.

The Pickens were eating supper in their apartment above the store. "Come in, Colby, and sit down. We're having leftover pashofa and fry bread from our tribal meeting today. Have some," said Mr. Pickens. Bert and his mother were seated across the table.

"No thanks, sir. I have to get home before dark. The pecans that I picked up today are on the scale outside. No need to disturb your supper. I'll collect my money tomorrow, or Bert can give it to me at school."

"Hold on a minute, Cole," said Bert, and he rose from the table and followed Colby down the stairs and out the back door. "What's wrong, man? You look like you've seen a ghost. Did the witch and her werewolf chase you again?"

"Cut the jokes, Bert. I didn't see anybody except Lucky, and he's no more werewolf than you are."

"Lucky? You mean that demon dog that ate the seat of my pants? Cole, get real. That dog is dangerous."

"How's your ankle?"

"Sore. Mom wrapped it with an elastic bandage. Dad was real mad at me over our Halloween prank. He says I'm not to go near the Weston Estate again. Not with you or anyone else. He says things are happening over there that we'd best leave alone."

"Yeah, but it's sure not vampire and werewolf stuff."

"What do you mean?"

Colby remained silent for a moment. "Promise you won't tell anybody? Swear?"

"Sure, Cole. I won't tell."

"Well, I found this and forty-nine others just like it," and Colby drew the plastic bag of marijuana from his jacket pocket.

Bert's eyes widened as Colby told him about the brush pile and the concealed stash, and how he had carefully replaced the leaves and twigs.

"Well, you'd better turn that in to the cops. You're gonna be in big trouble if you don't."

"I was thinking that if I catch the guy that hid it, maybe I'll get a reward or something. It will mean keeping watch on who goes over there. Can't you see the entrance to the Weston place from the front of your store? Maybe you could spy for me to see who goes up there."

"Lots of folks up to no good go there. But I'm not here all of the time – just on weekends. I guess Dad might keep a lookout for us if we ask him."

"Gosh, no. Don't tell your dad anything. Remember! You promised."

"Okay, Cole, but I think you're making a big mistake. That bag of weed is worth a lot of money. Some people would kill to get their hands on a stash like that."

"How do you know so much about it?"

Bert crossed his arms in front of his chest and pretended to look solemn, like a Hollywood Indian. "What you think Big Chief Pickens smoke in peace pipe, paleface?" Then he grinned.

"Cut out the jokes, Bert. Is that stuff really worth big money?"

"According to Chickasaw tom-toms and smoke signals, it's too hot for a kid like you to handle, Cole. Finding a big stash of marijuana is like finding loot from a bank robbery. Drug dealers and cops will get involved. Let me tell Dad. He'll know what to do."

"I need to think this over before I do anything. For now, Bert, just keep your mouth shut. We'll talk some more tomorrow."

Darkness hid the anxious expression on Colby's face as he pedaled his bicycle home. He was glad he had a friend like Bert to confide in.

The first thing Bert said when he re-entered the house was, "Guess what Colby found over on Weston Hill, Dad?"

Mr. Pickens' eyes opened wide, and his dark brown pupils looked like the holes of a shotgun barrel. "I wouldn't be surprised if he found a dead body." Then he pointed his fork at Bert and said, "Whatever he found, you leave it alone."

CHAPTER EIGHT

"Colby, where in the world have you been all afternoon? Your dad and I have been worried about you."

Colby shoved his hand into his jacket pocket to conceal the plastic bag. He hoped his eagle-eyed mother wouldn't notice. "Oh, I've been over on Weston Hill picking up pecans for some extra cash," he said casually. "I earned about thirty dollars today, and Mr. Kennedy offered me another paper route, so I told him I'd take it."

"Well, that's great, son," said Dad. "You've been such a help since I've been down with this bad back, but your mother and I still want to know where you are going and what you're doing – especially when you've been gone for several hours."

"I'm okay, Dad. You don't have to worry about me. I can take care of myself."

"We know we can rely on you to do the right thing, Colby. It's just that I feel we've lost touch. I promise that when my back heals, we'll go camping and fishing – be a real family again. Sorry you weren't around to watch the game with me. Cowboys beat the Bears. It was a great game!"

We'll probably never go camping again, Colby thought. Unless Dad has surgery, he'll be disabled and in pain for the rest of his life. Colby suspected that Tom was already addicted to pain killers. A year ago, his parents had energy and enthusiasm to spare. Now Dad was sallow and thin, almost skeletal. Deep creases slashed his face, and his eyes reminded Colby of windows in a haunted house.

His mother's beautiful hair was now streaked with gray, and instead of allowing it to fall into curls around her ears, she twisted it into a tight bun and shoved wavy tendrils under a cafeteria hairnet. Except on Sundays, Colby seldom saw her dressed in anything but a uniform.

Jeanie said, "It's late, Colby. You'll have to soak your hands in bleach to get rid of that pecan stain on your fingers. Be sure to use plenty of soap in the shower in case you touched poison ivy leaves in the woods. Your dad and I have already eaten supper, but I'll warm yours in the microwave. Are you hungry?"

"Always, Mom, always."

"There's leftover roast and mashed potatoes and some fruit salad in the fridge. How's that? I'll fix your plate while you take a shower."

Anxious that his observant mother might notice the plastic bag of marijuana in his jacket pocket or smell its contents, Colby sidled out of the room and hurried down the hall to his room. He turned on the shower. Then he hung up his jacket and removed his clothes, which he tossed into the hamper. He tried to think of a good place to hide the plastic bag so that his mother would not find it. She seldom came into his room now because Colby changed the sheets on his bed, ran the sweeper, and did his own laundry, but he was taking no chances. He stuffed the plastic bag into the toe of one of his cowboy boots and shoved it into a corner of his closet.

As he soaped his body and shampooed his hair, he congratulated himself on his cleverness. He had covered the black plastic garbage bag with leaves and twigs and placed the string marker so carefully that whoever put it there would never know he'd found their cache. That is, unless they counted the small plastic bags. Forty-nine of them, and he had number fifty in the toe of his boot. No one knew about the stash except Bert and whoever hid it there.

He stepped from the shower and dried his hair. Then he buffed his body with a rough towel until his skin tingled. As he pulled on a clean tee shirt and shorts, he noticed that his hands were scratched and stained brown by tannic acid from the pecan hulls. He poured a little bleach into the sink and scrubbed off some of the stain. Then he sniffed his palms to see if they were tainted with the scent of marijuana. Not a trace.

After eating his supper, he finished five algebra problems and read his assignment in *Great Expectations*, a Victorian novel by Charles Dickens. Most of his classmates hated it, but Colby liked it. Each character's life was twisted and linked by life's misfortunes. Colby wished a benefactor would leave him lots of money – somebody like Miss Havisham, the mysterious old recluse, or Magwich, the escaped criminal who'd become rich in Australia. He knew he would never spend money as foolishly as Philip Pirrup – Pip – who wants to become a gentleman and impress Estella, the stuck-up girl he adores.

On the other hand, the marijuana cache could possibly become the source of his own "great expectations." Maybe a car. Dalton Barrett's black Corvette had impressed Linda, for sure. Should he sell the stuff and pay for things his Mom and Dad needed? Should he tell the police and hope for a reward? Should he do nothing – just spy and find out who hid the stash?

The next morning during band practice, he tried to talk to Linda, but Mr. Davis tapped his baton on his metal music stand each time they began to whisper. After class as they packed their trombones in their cases, Colby said, "Did your dad tell you I came by yesterday?"

"No, but I suppose he told you his new rule. No dates, no boys at the house, and no phone calls for a month. He was very angry after what happened Friday night."

"What happened? Was he mad because of Dalton's kiss at the homecoming game?"

"Well, he didn't like it, but the worst thing was" – she looked down at the toe of her shoe – "I didn't get home until 2 A.M." Colby frowned and followed Linda out of the band room and into the crowded and noisy hallway to her locker.

"For pete's sake! Why not? The dance was over at 12. Did Dalton's car break down?"

Linda giggled and said, "No. We..."

Suddenly two muscular arms slammed Linda's locker door shut and pinned her against it. Dalton Barrett's broad back effectively blocked Colby from seeing the expression on her face.

Dalton spoke over his shoulder to Colby. "Two's company; three's a crowd, kid, so beat it! This little gal and I need to have a private talk." Placing his arm protectively around Linda's shoulders, the tall, handsome senior steered her down the hall. Dalton whispered something in her ear that made her laugh.

Colby clenched his fists. He wanted to grab Dalton by the shoulder, whirl him around, and punch him in the mouth, even if it meant getting two black eyes! What satisfaction! To wipe that egotistical smile off "Darling" Dalton's face. But fighting at school meant he'd get expelled. Cool it, he thought. Red-faced and frustrated, he turned and walked in the opposite direction.

Melissa Marshall stepped out of a nearby classroom and blocked his way. She must have heard the whole thing. "Colby, you're too nice a kid to take that stuff from Dalton Barrett or from her. Linda's not worth it." She smiled. "If you ever need a shoulder to cry on, remember me."

The bell rang for second period, so Colby dashed down the hall to class. Mrs. McPherson was already checking roll.

"You're tardy, Colby," she said.

"Sorry," he mumbled and hurried down the aisle to his seat.

During discussion of *Great Expectations*, Colby gazed out of the window. Maybe Linda just didn't realize how much he loved her. How could any girl be interested in a conceited phony like Dalton? Maybe he could talk to her at lunch. But no. He'd told Bert to meet him behind the gym to discuss what to do about the marijuana stash. He'd have to write Linda a note, but how could he ever say what was in his heart on a piece of paper?

Mary Kennedy, who sat behind him, poked him in the back with her pencil eraser.

"Colby. Colby Elliott!" Mrs. McPherson was speaking.

"Huh? Yes, Ma'am?"

"Where is your mind, Colby? Being tardy was bad enough, but your lack of attention in class will not do. Wake up! The office assistant has brought this note that says you are to report to Mr. Pembroke's office immediately." Other students snickered as Colby arose from his desk and left the classroom.

Through the glass door of the principal's office, he could see Mr. Pembroke talking to a policeman. A large German shepherd, panting and dripping saliva from his lolling tongue, lay on the floor beside his master, observing his every move.

"Come in, Colby," said Mr. Pembroke in a cold, impersonal tone. "We want to ask you a few questions." Colby stood at attention in front of the principal's desk. "As you know, we routinely ask the drug squad to bring their dogs to sniff out any illegal drugs circulating at the school. This morning Officer Reed made a sweep through the halls with his dog, and where do you suppose the dog stopped? At your locker. Now this was quite a surprise. As far as I know, Colby, you've always been a model student, and it's possible that the dog has made a mistake. Isn't that right, Officer Reed?"

"Yes, sir, but his nose seldom misses a sign," said Reed.

Colby felt as if his legs had turned into rubber bands. But he wasn't ready to confide anything to these men about the valuable stash that he'd found near the Weston Estate. They'd probably think it was his. How could that dog smell a plastic bag of marijuana hidden in the toe of his boot in a closet twelve blocks away? Surreptitiously, Colby rubbed his hand across his face and sniffed his own palm. It still had the lingering odor of bleach. He shoved his hands into his jeans pocket.

"Sir, I don't have any illegal drugs in my locker," he said.

"We'd like for you to open your locker for confirmation of that, Colby. I hope that you're telling us the truth." When Mr. Pembroke made eye contact with him, Colby felt like a bird being hypnotized by a cobra.

The two men, the dog, and Colby walked toward his locker. No one was in the hallway, but some of the classroom doors were open, and students and teachers knew what the officer and the dog were there for. Whispers started when they saw Colby with them.

Colby opened his locker and took out his jacket first. The dog went berserk, whining and barking, as he sniffed the jacket. The officer examined the jacket closely, searching the lining and feeling inside each pocket. He removed the roach clip that the tire slasher had dropped and looked accusingly at Colby.

"What about this little item?" he asked.

Colby told them about his slashed bicycle tires and finding the clip, but he knew that Officer Reed and Mr. Pembroke didn't believe him. Then Colby emptied his locker of each textbook and notebook. The dog was interested only in the jacket.

"Well, son, we've found nothing more incriminating than this suspicious roach clip, but my dog definitely smells the scent of marijuana on your jacket. Have you been hanging out with someone else who smokes marijuana? Are you sure you have nothing to tell us?" asked Officer Reed.

"No, Sir," he answered. He had felt like this once before during a junior high football game when he held the ball aloft, ready to throw a pass. Suddenly a huge lineman loomed in front of him, ready to block the pass and grind him into the dirt. He'd dodged, kept the ball, and run for a touchdown. He decided to dodge Mr. Pembroke and Officer Reed and go for the touchdown. That marijuana cache was too valuable to give up so easily. He looked down at the dog and started to pet him.

"Don't touch my dog, kid. He might bite, just like I will if I find out you are lying," said Officer Reed.

Frowning, Mr. Pembroke said, "If you know something about drug deals, or if you are taking drugs, Colby, you need help. Officer Reed says someone gave him a tip that a student at Bartlett High School is distributing marijuana. We have no evidence that you are involved or have done anything wrong, except for that clip and the dog's reaction. However, I am going to call your parents and make an appointment for some counseling sessions. Now go back to class, and I'll talk to you later."

CHAPTER NINE

"You weren't dumb enough to bring that plastic bag of weed to school, were you, Cole?" asked Bert. "When I saw Officer Reed and his dog with you in the hall, I just knew you were busted."

"Naw, I left it at home, but that drug dog smelled the roach clip in my jacket pocket. What a nose! I never believed those dogs could really do that until today. How do druggies get away with it?"

"The way dopers look and act usually gives them away – you know – red-eyed, strung out, sleepy or flying high, different symptoms. But most drug dealers look and act like ordinary folks. Like you, Colby. You'd never suspect them except they suddenly have lots of money to spend – real flush, with new clothes, or a new car. You wonder where they got it."

"Well, I haven't become a user or a seller," Colby said. "Funny thing, though, Officer Reed said that he brought the dog to school because he got a tip about a student who is peddling marijuana. You're the only one who knows that I found the stash, Bert, and I haven't sold any of it, so somebody else at Bartlett High must be peddling pot."

"If you don't tell the cops what you know, Cole, you are going to be in big trouble with the law and maybe with the person who hid the stuff on Weston Hill. If it was me, I'd rather have Officer Reed on my case any day than some drug dealer."

"Mr. Pembroke threatened to call my folks for a session with the counselor. How can he do that? Dad and Mom can't come running up to school just because the drug dog sniffed my jacket. Reed didn't find anything in my locker. So far, I haven't done anything wrong except pick up somebody else's roach clip and keep my mouth shut about the pack rat's nest on Weston Hill. Why should I tell them what I know? I intend to catch whoever hid the stuff. Then I'll turn them in to Reed."

"I think it's a dumb idea. Even if you find out who hid it, what good will it do?"

"I'll report them. I'll be a witness. Maybe I'll get a reward. If I just turn the stuff in, whoever hid it can deny they know anything about it – maybe even say it's mine."

"If you tell the cops, they'll stake out the place and be official witnesses. If you try to do it yourself, you might get in the way of a drug bust."

"What about this idea? I'll hide in one of those big pecan trees and spy on whoever comes to claim that stuff in the pack rat's nest. Then maybe the drug dealer will pay to keep me quiet. At least I'll get something out of it."

"That's blackmail! What are you gonna do, Cole? Sit in a tree twenty-four hours a day? Those drug dealers will probably sneak in there after dark. And what about your paper route? You gonna give it up to sit in a tree? Take my advice, old buddy. Tell Reed."

"If I tell the cops about it, I won't get anything but a pat on the back. They probably won't believe I'm innocent since I didn't tell them about it this morning."

"Better a pat on the back than a hole in the head, Colby. That marijuana stash is worth a lot of money, and drug dealers are bad to the bone."

"Well, maybe you're right, Bert. If I tell Officer Reed about it this afternoon, will you go down to the station with me and back up my story?"

Bert avoided looking at Colby. "Not this afternoon, Cole. Dad's expecting me to help out at the store."

Colby knew he was innocent, but somehow he felt guilty because he hadn't told Officer Reed about the drug cache. Now he was afraid to take the marijuana packets to the police. As a suspect, he couldn't sell them, for sure. He decided his only option was to discover who hid the stash and turn them in. He trusted Bert, but he wondered if Bert really could keep a secret. Would he spill the secret to his dad? Or maybe tell his cousin Eddie?

After school, Colby folded and stuffed the *Bartlett Banner* into plastic sleeves and threw papers onto his customers' porches as fast as he could. When the Banner hit Linda's front porch, someone looked out from behind the curtain, and Linda ran out on the porch.

"I can't talk but a minute, Colby. Daddy will be home soon, and if he catches me talking to Dalton or any boy – even you – I'll be grounded for another month." She thrust a small package tied with a blue satin ribbon at Colby. "Read this note and you'll understand."

"Why is your dad mad at me? What have I done?"

"Nothing. He just doesn't understand how teenagers feel when they're in love. Read the note." Linda turned and raced back toward the house. At the door, she paused momentarily and blew Colby a goodbye kiss. "Friends forever, Colby!"

Joy warmed Colby's heart as he stuffed the package into his pocket. He popped a wheelie and zoomed off down the street. At the corner he passed Mr. Jenkins's car, headed home. Linda's father scowled at him in recognition. I'll think of a way to make the old geezer trust me, Colby thought.

Linda's note burned like fire in his pocket. He couldn't wait to read it, so he stopped at the park and propped his bicycle against a tree. Nearby, several children were screaming with excitement as they swooshed down the slide and rocked the teeter totter. He sat on a bench near the tennis court, where two girls were lobbing a ball back and forth across the net. When one of them yelled, "Hey, Colby!" he recognized Melissa and Pam and waved to them.

He untied the ribbon that bound the package. Linda's pink note paper smelled like roses. It was folded around something wrapped in a tissue. The blue glass ring fell out. He remembered the day he gave the ring to her – the noisy midway, the fumes from diesel engines that powered the rides, loud music from the merry-go-round's calliope, smells of hot dogs and cotton candy, and Linda's kiss after he placed the ring on her finger. With trembling fingers, Colby opened the note and read.

Dear Colby,

Here is your ring back. Dalton has asked me to go steady. He's going to give me a promise ring as soon as Daddy lets me go on dates again. When you are older, you will understand what real love is.
Friends forever.
Linda

Instead of a fall day decorated with blue sky and gold and orange leaves, Colby suddenly saw a gray and dead world. He felt like screaming and crying at the same time. The crumpled note fell from his hand, and he tossed the cheap ring into the bushes. Understand? Old enough to understand? Linda was the one who did not understand.

Why couldn't she see what a conceited jerk Dalton Barrett was? Did a guy have to drive a fancy black sports car and buy a girl an expensive promise ring before she would appreciate his adoration? Numb with grief, Colby stared off into space, unaware of time passing.

A hand waved slowly back and forth in front of his face, and Melissa said, "Are you okay, Cole? You act like you've been hit by a truck."

"Sure. I'm okay," he mumbled and rose from the bench like a punchy boxer.

"Pam and I are taking these little rug rats to Burger Bob's for supper," she said. "Chain your bike to the swing set and come with us. We need a man to help us herd these gremlins. Their parents are off on a Caribbean cruise, and we are their nannies! We're buying the burgers – expense account, you know."

Glad that somebody wanted him – even to baby-sit, he helped the girls load the rowdy children into their parents' van and climbed in with them. In such lively company, he couldn't brood in silence over his broken love affair.

After supper, Pam walked outside to watch the children climb on Burger Bob's jungle gym and tumble in the red, white and blue bubble pit. Across a table, littered with catsup packets and mashed fries, Melissa and Colby talked.

"Whose kids are those, Melissa?"

"They belong to Dr. Perry and his wife Julie. She's a lawyer with a busy practice. I live with them. Doc and Julie adopted me after Mother and Daddy were killed in a crash on a California freeway. I was just a kid." Melissa shook her head as if to erase the memory. "Mom and Dad were high school classmates of the Perrys. They were best friends. After they graduated from Bartlett High, my folks went to California to work, and Doc and Julie went to college."

As she talked, Melissa began cleaning the debris from the table. "I lived in several foster homes in California and was real close to messing up my life when Doc and Julie came and got me. I'd do anything for them."

"Gosh, Melissa, don't you have any other relatives?"

"No. Just Doc and Julie and Alan and Annie, their kids."

"Dr. Perry is my dad's doctor. I've never met him, though."

"Well, he's got lots of patients. You know how doctors and lawyers are always on call – night and day. I take care of Annie and Alan when Doc and Julie are away from home. *Au pair* is the fancy name for my job as a nanny. I have my own room and nice clothes and anything else I need. They even pay me a salary. I'm saving my money for college next year."

"Sounds like they really trust you," said Colby.

"I try not to do anything to disappoint them. This week they're off on a vacation cruise. While they're gone, Pam is helping me. We fix the kids' breakfast and put them on the school bus and head for school ourselves. Then Pam and I rush back to the house before the school bus brings them home. We do the laundry and either fix supper or go out for burgers, like tonight. After the kids go to bed, we do our homework. We even have an expense account to buy groceries and gasoline for the van if we need it. It's a wonderful job!"

"The Perrys sure give you a lot of responsibility," said Colby.

"Oh, I've helped take care of their kids for a couple of years. Alan and Annie are like my little brother and sister."

Talking to Melissa and playing with the children made Colby temporarily forget Linda's note and his own heartache. When Melissa and Pam dropped him off at the park to pick up his bike, Melissa put her arm around his shoulders and said, "Here, Colby, you dropped this." Then she removed the crumpled pink notepaper and ribbon from her pocket and placed them in his hand. "Maybe you'll want to paste it in your scrapbook. Believe me, kiddo, someday you'll laugh about stuff like this." To his surprise, she hugged him and planted a kiss on his cheek.

On the way home, he wondered why Dalton Barrett had spread nasty rumors about Melissa to the guys in the locker room – that she took drugs, and when she was high, she'd do things that made Colby blush. She seemed unaware that her reputation at Bartlett High was lower than a snake's belly. He wondered what Melissa had ever seen in Dalton when they were dating. Did she date Travis now, or were they together at the homecoming dance just because he was her escort during the homecoming celebration? Colby decided that he had a lot to learn about women.

CHAPTER TEN

"Where in the world have you been, Colby?" asked Jeanie. "I called Pickens' store, and I called Mr. Kennedy at the paper, and when I couldn't locate you... ." She burst into tears.

He stepped quickly to her side. "What's wrong, Mom? What's happened?"

Jeanie wiped her eyes with a tissue and said, "Your dad's in bed sleeping off an overdose of those pain pills. When I got home from work, I couldn't wake him up. I called Dr. Perry, but his nurse told me he's on vacation, so she sent a physician's assistant to the house, and he gave Tom fluids intravenously and some medicine to counteract the pills he took. Mr. Sanders – yes, that's his name – wanted to call an ambulance, but I told him we couldn't afford it. When he left, he said that Tom was stable and resting, but we're supposed to wake him every hour to make sure he's all right. If things get worse in the night, we're supposed to call the emergency room at the hospital." She paced back and forth. "Oh, I wish Dr. Perry was here. He'd know exactly what to do." She started to cry again.

"Come sit down, Mom. I'll make you a cup of hot tea. Have you had any supper?"

"Oh, I couldn't eat a bite, honey, but the tea would help."

He put the kettle on the burner, looked in the refrigerator for leftovers, but found nothing but some eggs, so he scrambled those and popped bread into the toaster. He fixed a tray for his mother and returned to the living room, where he found Jeanie lying on the couch. Her face and eyes were swollen from crying.

"Here, Mom. You need to eat something. I put sugar in the tea." Colby pulled up a stool and sat in front of her.

"Dr. Perry's assistant asked me if Tom had been depressed. He wanted to know if I had found a note. He must have suspected suicide, but he just doesn't know Tom like I do. I explained about the accident and how much pain Tom has endured since last summer, and I showed him the pills that Dr. Perry prescribed. He said that since some were left in the bottle, Tom probably didn't realize how many he had taken and just accidentally overdosed. A person bent on suicide would have taken them all."

"Dad needs that operation, Mom. Isn't there any way we can arrange it? He can't go on like this."

"Well, the charity hospital in the city might take him, but I would be afraid to trust just any surgeon to operate on him. Dr. Perry says the operation might cure his back problem, or it could paralyze him. It's touch and go. He needs a specialist."

"Would he have to go to the city for surgery?"

"Maybe not. Dr. Perry has been driving to the city once a week to assist a famous orthopedic surgeon and learn his techniques. Maybe he'll be able to operate on Tom soon. I would have to take an unpaid leave-of-absence from my job, and we just don't have money for an extended out-of-town hospital stay."

"Can't you borrow the money, Mom? Won't somebody who knows us lend us the money?"

"We're already in debt up to our ears, Colby." She looked tired and desperate. "Our unpaid medical bills are huge. We've applied for Social Security disability payments, and when that comes through, maybe I can stop working and stay home to take care of Tom. The house is mortgaged to the hilt, and payments are due. I'm at my wit's end." She began to cry again.

"Finish your eggs and toast, Mom, and take a hot shower. I'll clean up the kitchen and sit with Dad. You need to rest if you are going to sit with him when he wakes up."

Colby unloaded clean dishes from the dishwasher and reloaded it. Then he went into the bedroom where his father slept on a rented hospital bed. With his head thrown back, Tom Elliott looked like a corpse, rather than the handsome, vigorous man he had once been. His dry lips were parted, and his sandy hair was tousled. A stubble of beard on his thin face made him look unkempt and vulnerable. He breathed deeply, as though each breath were his last.

Colby switched on the reading lamp beside the bed. Like an evil omen, a white envelope with the school's letterhead lay on the table with the flap opened. Colby read the letter.

Dear Parent or Guardian of Colby Elliott:
Your child has exhibited negative behavior at school that indicates a need for a parent-teacher conference. Please telephone the school at your earliest convenience to make an appointment with the counselor.
Amos Pembroke, Principal
Bartlett High School

Colby felt sick when he realized that his father had read the letter. The last thing that Tom Elliott needed was a son with problems at school. Why couldn't Mr. Pembroke and Officer Reed mind their own business? They had convicted him without proof. Maybe they need to check somebody else's locker – somebody with flashy clothes and a new car.

But Colby had to admit that after word got around school that Officer Reed and the drug dog had inspected his locker, some of the dopers had suddenly become very friendly. Strung-out stoners and crackheads who lacked interest in anything except getting the next joint or rock kept asking him what kind of drugs he had for sale. He knew he could peddle fifty packets of marijuana easily, and the money would relieve his family's financial crisis. He could make the mortgage payment and buy Dad a little time in the hospital. But how could he explain the sudden windfall of cash?

Jeanie emerged from the bathroom in her gown and fuzzy red bathrobe. She stood beside Tom and held his hand.

"Go lie down, Mom. I'll sleep here on the cot beside Dad. If he wakes up, I'll call you. You'll need lots of rest for tomorrow."

"You need your rest, too, Colby. Tomorrow's a school day."

"Hey, I'll sleep when I'm old," he said, projecting an optimism that he did not really feel. His mother smiled half-heartedly and went to bed.

Sometime in the night, Tom Elliot awoke, and Colby gave him a cool drink of water. "Are you okay, Dad?"

"I feel like my body's turned to stone, son. Where's your mother? What's happened?"

"The doctor says you took too many pain pills. Here, drink some more water. You need to drink lots of liquids to flush that medicine from your body."

"God help me. Sometimes I just lose heart."

"Do you want me to get Mom?"

"No, let her rest. She works so hard, and I'm just a burden."

"She loves you, Dad, and so do I."

Tears came to Tom's eyes, and he gripped Colby's hand.

"If I don't make it through this valley of shadows, son, I know I can count on you to be a man and help your mother. Up to now, you've never given us a minute of worry." A guilty look crossed Colby's face as he glanced toward the letter on the table.

Tom noticed and said, "What's all this about 'negative behavior' at school, son? You've never had any problems before."

"Don't worry, Dad. It's all a mistake. I can handle it myself, so just forget it. Now try to get a little rest."

The next morning as he dressed for school, Colby listened to his dad groan as he rose from the bed and braced his hips against the stainless steel bed railings. "Better use my wheel chair this morning, Jeanie. My head feels like somebody hit me with a baseball bat."

"Drink this coffee," she said. "I'm not going to work today. Mr. Sanders, the physician's assistant, said he'd come by about 7:30 before he makes his rounds at the hospital. He said he wants to try some new pain medicine that is less addictive and more effective than what you've been taking."

"I'm so ashamed, Jeanie. When the pain gets so bad, I don't have good sense. You and Colby – I've ruined your lives. Sometimes it seems hopeless that I'll ever be a whole man again. Colby's such a great kid. And you're still young and pretty. You deserve more than this."

"Now you stop that! Colby and I couldn't live without you. When Dr. Perry comes back from his vacation, we are going to find a way to repair your back." She plumped his pillow and straightened the cover. "How about waffles and sausage for breakfast?" she said and smiled.

For the first time, Colby realized that he was not the only actor in the family. His mother hid her feelings too. In the kitchen, he slathered peanut butter and jelly on two pieces of bread, gulped a glass of milk, and stuffed an apple into his pocket.

"I'm off," he said and rushed out the back door.

Since he was almost late, he abandoned the bicycle path and cut through the student parking lot. Travis, Eddie, and three other seniors were admiring Dalton's black Corvette. As Colby pedaled by, Dalton slammed the hood shut. "How'd you like to race me, sonny," he said, and the others laughed. Red-faced, Colby pretended to ignore them.

He entered the building and hurried toward the principal's office to tell Mr. Pembroke that his parents would be unable to keep their appointment with the counselor, but Mr. Pembroke had gone to an administrator's conference in the city.

A secretary, who didn't bother to get up from her desk, said, "Sign the book, so Mr. Pembroke will know you've stopped by." She didn't notice that Colby scrawled Philip Pirrup instead of his own name. He was sure she'd never connect that name with the hero of Dickens' *Great Expectations*. He would straighten things out with Mr. Pembroke later.

On the way down the hall, he passed Dalton pressing Linda against her locker in an ardent embrace. Hot waves of outrage prompted him to say something sarcastic, but he stifled the urge. As he stalked past them, he wished a teacher would see that performance and put both Dalton and Linda in detention.

CHAPTER ELEVEN

When Colby got home that afternoon, he could smell roast beef seasoned with garlic and bay leaves cooking in the crockpot. His mom and dad were concentrating on a game of pinochle at the kitchen table.

"How'd things go today, son?" asked Tom.

"No problem. How about you?"

"Much, much better. Having your mother at home today has cured what ails me. When Nurse Jeanie holds my hand, my aches and pains vanish."

Jeanie smiled. "Mr. Sanders gave your dad a new prescription to control his muscle spasms."

"Yeah. As long as I don't try to dance the tango with your mom, I'm fairly comfortable. Sanders tells me that Dr. Perry will be back from his vacation soon, and he set up an appointment for me."

"We're having pot roast for supper in about an hour, Colby, and cherry pie."

"Mmm, mmm. My favorites. Since everything's okay here, Mom, I think I'll run over to Bert's for a while. Need any milk or bread? I can get it at Pickens' store."

"Well, yes. Bring a half gallon of milk. We'll eat about 6:30, so don't be late," she said.

"You know, it's high time this family shared a meal," said Tom. "We haven't sat down at the table together in ages." He asked, "Do you need money for the milk, son?"

Colby jingled coins in his pants pocket. "Today was pay day. See you at supper."

He wheeled between cars parked in front of Pickens' Trading Post, chained his bike to the fence, and entered the store. Mr. Pickens was busy at the cash register, making change for a customer, and Bert was sacking groceries.

"Got a minute, Bert?" Colby asked. "I'm gonna run over to Weston hill to check that pack rat's nest. Want to go with me?"

"No can do. I'll be busy here for another hour helping Dad."

"I'll be back about dark to give you the lowdown. My bike's chained to your fence."

"You're making a mistake, Cole. Better leave that pack rat's nest alone."

"Maybe so, but I've got a hunch it's time for the rats to show up again to claim their stuff. See ya later."

Mr. Pickens peered over his Benjamin Franklin glasses at Colby's back as he left the store. "Watch the register, Bert. I'll be right back," he said, and he stepped into the alcove where the telephone was located.

As Colby strolled down the lane bordering the Weston estate, he picked up a stick and lopped off the heads of dead sunflowers lining the weedy path. Then he ran the stick along the iron fence, making a loud racket. No sign of Lucky.

When he reached the dead log where the marijuana cache was hidden, he scanned the ground for footprints or signs that someone else had been there. Dead leaves and twigs were untouched, and the piece of string lay in the same place.

He continued walking to the crest of Weston Hill, where a huge pecan tree grew inside the fence with its strong limbs jutting out in all directions. In spite of Mr. Pickens' warning not to trespass beyond the fence, Colby decided to climb the tree. It would be a good hiding place to spy on the drug dealers if they came for their loot.

Careful not to snag his jeans, he vaulted over the spiked iron fence and shinnied up the trunk, scratching his hands and face on the tree's rough bark. Then he settled himself comfortably with his back against the trunk and his legs stretched out on a large limb. From the crotch of the tree, he got a spectacular view of farms and ranches in the nearby valley. Directly below him at the edge of the pecan orchard, he saw what Miss Weston must have meant by trespassers "poaching." Someone had cultivated and harvested marijuana plants just outside the fence on her estate. A few dead stalks, stripped of their leaves, were all that remained.

He sat on the limb for nearly an hour. He'd heard of deer hunters dozing off in tree stands and falling to the ground, so he swung his legs, back and forth, to stay alert. Then he heard the dog's bark, growing louder as he approached. Colby sat very still. The dog sniffed the ground under the tree. Then he looked up and began barking. Colby knew how a treed raccoon must feel. With ears and tail erect, and bearing his weight on his hind legs, Lucky scratched at the tree trunk with front paws and jumped upward as if he'd like to climb it.

"Hey, Lucky, old buddy. Remember me?"

"Bark! Bark! Bark! Bark! Whine."

"It's me! Your pal, Cole."

The agitated dog continued to bark and whine. He ran around the tree again and reared up on his hind legs and scratched at the bark.

"Doncha even know me? Remember? I'm the guy that gave you the jerky." Colby wished he'd brought a doggy treat.

Not an expert at reading the dog's body language, Colby wasn't sure how to interpret Lucky's barks and whines. He didn't seem as vicious as he had on previous occasions. His ears were not laid back and his bark seemed more curious and playful than angry.

If dogs could talk, Colby hoped Lucky was saying, "Come on down, kid. Let's be pals," but he was afraid to trust that feeling. After all, he was trespassing, and he hadn't forgotten the dog's speed and agility or razor sharp teeth when Miss Weston turned him loose on Halloween. If provoked, Lucky could kill.

After a while, the dog realized that the trespasser wasn't coming down, so he stretched out on leaves beneath the tree's canopy and waited. In the dim light, Colby could see him panting, with his long red tongue lolled out and dripping saliva. Occasionally, he gazed up at Colby with an expression that seemed friendly, but every time Colby tried to descend, the dog began to bark.

Then Colby got an idea. He unlaced one of his sneakers and held it aloft. "Here, boy." Colby showed Lucky the shoe. With his ears pointed forward and muscles ready for action, the alert dog watched Colby, who pretended to throw the shoe. The dog made a false start but checked himself. Then Colby said, "Fetch, Lucky," and he threw the shoe as far away from the tree and fence as he could.

The second that Lucky bounded in pursuit of the sneaker, Colby shinnied down the tree and ran for the fence. Just as he was vaulting over it, Lucky returned with the shoe in his strong jaws and held it up for Colby to take.

I can't believe this, thought Colby, but he cautiously reached for the shoe, and Lucky dropped it into his hand. The dog lunged and barked, indicating that he wanted to play the fetch game again, so once again, Colby hurled the shoe between the trees.

"You've played this fetch game many times, haven't you, boy? All it took to win you over were a few bites of jerky, some kind words, and a game of fetch. Maybe others did the same – like whoever planted that marijuana. The only person who can really turn you into an attack dog is Miss Weston."

When Lucky returned the shoe the third time, Colby dared pat him on the head. The dog returned affection with tail wags and whines. Suddenly, as if Lucky heard a signal, inaudible to Colby, the dog turned and ran toward the gloomy mansion.

"Friends forever, Lucky," called Colby. He pulled on the sneaker, still wet from the dog's saliva, and walked down the lane toward Pickens' store.

It was almost dark when he got there. To his surprise, the familiar black Corvette was parked in the drive. Colby could see someone scrunched down in the back seat. He didn't want to start any trouble with Dalton or Travis, so he walked around to the side of the building where his bicycle was chained.

Bragging loudly to Mr. Pickens about how they'd won district for the Bulldogs, Dalton and Travis emerged from the store, each with a six pack of beer. They slammed their car doors, and Dalton peeled out of the graveled driveway. Colby watched the car glide across Delmonte and turn into Weston Road, where he imagined they would drink beer and toss the empty cans into the ditch.

He decided not to tell Bert about his adventure with Lucky. After the way things had turned out, he wished he hadn't told him about the marijuana cache. Ever since Halloween night, when Lucky ripped the seat of his pants, Bert had refused to go with him to Weston Hill. He claimed that his dad ruled the Weston Estate off limits, but Colby thought that was just an excuse. Bert kept warning him not to get involved with the drug dealers, and urging him to talk to Officer Reed, but when Colby asked him to go to the police station with him, Bert said he had other plans and didn't want to get involved. Colby and Bert had been friends for a long time, but "friends forever" didn't mean much to Linda, and Colby wondered about Bert. Wouldn't it be a hoot if Lucky turned out to be his only friend?

When Colby entered the store to purchase milk for his mother, Bert said, "I watched you as you cross the street. Anything changed over on the hill?"

"Nope. Things were pretty quiet. Just Miss Weston's guard dog on patrol."

"That dog's dangerous. You won't catch me trespassing again."

For the first time ever, an awkward silence separated the boys. Then Bert said, "I guess you saw Dalton and Travis leave. They were headed over there to drink beer. Everybody knows they broke Coach's training rules during football season, but now that football's over, they guzzle beer like water and smoke like chimneys. Dad doesn't like to sell it to them, but they're eighteen and have IDs."

"I'm glad I didn't meet them on Weston Hill. I could hold my own in a fight with one of them but not both. They had somebody else in the car with them."

The clock on the wall behind the counter chimed the half hour. "Oh, gosh. I promised to be home by 6:30 for supper. Give me a half gallon of milk, Bert, and I'll be on my way." Colby placed money on the counter.

Bert sacked a carton of milk and slipped a small box of chocolate covered cherries into the bag. "Those are for your dad, Cole. I hope he gets better real soon."

Late evening traffic on Delmonte was heavy, so Colby rode his bicycle close to the curb. Suddenly someone honked so insistently behind him that he almost lost his balance. The black Corvette whizzed past, and as it went by, Travis Turner rolled down the passenger window and with his middle finger shot an obscene gesture at Colby.

"Get off the street and onto the sidewalk where tricycles and punk kids like you belong!" Travis shouted.

Dalton, the driver, nearly sideswiped another car as he swerved into the left lane. The Corvette sped down the street with Dalton honking the Bartlett High signal, two shorts and a long beep. Nervous drivers moved over to let him pass. The person scrunched down in the back seat turned and looked through the rear window with large, frightened eyes. It was Linda.

She's headed for trouble, Colby thought. I'll bet her dad doesn't know she's hanging out with those guys. Disappointment and anger made him pedal faster.

Tom and Jeanie were already eating supper when Colby entered the kitchen. "We waited for you," said Jeanie, "but the food was getting cold, so we started without you."

"Yeah, we waited for you like one pig waits for another," Tom joked, a verbal signal to Colby that he was feeling much better.

"Sorry, Mom. No excuse." Colby washed his hands at the sink and sat down.

"Now that Colby's here, let's ask God's blessing for this wonderful meal." They joined hands and bowed their heads. Then Tom said, "God of grace and Creator of all good things, we thank you for the love we share. We thank you for all the happy times we've had together. Speak to our hearts and guide our actions. Be with us when life tests us with difficult choices. Give comfort and hope to those who are lonely tonight. And we especially thank you for this abundant supper. Amen."

"Amen," said Colby.

CHAPTER TWELVE

The next afternoon, Colby threw his paper route and headed for the Bartlett police station. He'd made a decision. Peddling drugs was wrong, no matter how desperately he needed the money. In spite of the consequences, he intended to tell Officer Reed the truth about his discovery and to surrender the packet of grass, still hidden in his boot.

Maybe if he volunteered as an undercover drug agent at Bartlett High, Officer Reed would overlook the fact he'd kept the pack rat's nest a secret. He really didn't like the idea of being a snitch, but ever since the day Officer Reed searched his locker, many of his classmates thought he was a drug dealer. Dopers kept accosting him in the halls, begging him to sell them some "weed." A few even asked him for "crack." The more he denied that he had drugs for sale, the more money they offered. Colby could not believe how widespread the drug problem had become at Bartlett High, and he wanted to help stop it.

When he entered the police station, phones were ringing, and a uniformed dispatcher was giving directions over the radio to another officer somewhere in a squad car. From a stainless steel cart, a trustee in bright orange overalls was serving supper trays to prisoners behind bars. Colby could see piles of rice and red beans in compartments on plastic trays, with bowls of peaches and cartons of milk on the side. It smelled good. Down a corridor, a prisoner in the drunk tank kept shouting, "Lemme outa here! I know my rights!"

At last a policewoman came to the desk. Instead of looking like a tough crime fighter, sworn to uphold law and order on the streets of Bartlett, she reminded Colby of a matronly grandmother, plump and smiling.

"May I help you, sir?" she said. Her blue eyes looked large and friendly.

"I'd like to speak to Officer Reed."

"Sorry, young man. He's gone to deliver a prisoner to the Washita County jail, and he won't be back on duty here, officially, that is, until tomorrow. May I take a message or be of assistance?"

"Well, no, ma'am. I just need to talk to Officer Reed."

"Could another officer help you? That's what we're here for, you know." She smiled.

"No, thank you, ma'am. My business is with Officer Reed."

"Well, then, may I have your name and address so that I can tell him you came by? Official report, you know." She picked up a pen and began to write down the time and date.

Colby thought fast. It had taken plenty of nerve for him to come here in the first place, and he surely didn't want to spill what he knew about the marijuana stash to a stranger, policewoman or not. What if she arrests me and throws me in jail? he thought,

"Uh, I'll come back tomorrow," he said, and to avoid making eye contact with her, he gazed at the clock on the wall.

"But what is your name, young man?" The policewoman looked at him intently, as though to memorize his features.

"Philip Pirrup," he lied. Then he turned and walked quickly toward the heavy doors. The policewoman's eyes seemed to bore a hole between his shoulder blades. Escaping prisoners must feel like this, he thought.

As he unchained his bicycle from the rack outside the station, a car drove up, and who should emerge but Mr. Pickens and his nephew Eddie Imotichey? Colby turned his back and ducked his head, but they did not even glance toward him as they entered the station.

That squealer, Bert! he thought. I'll bet he told his dad about the marijuana stash, and now they're here to report it. I'll never convince Officer Reed I didn't intend to sell it. Colby was glad he hadn't talked to Reed.

On the way home, he passed Dr. Perry's house, a three story Victorian mansion built during the Oklahoma oil boom of the 1930s by Judge Henry Bartlett, the town's founder. Albert Weston had built his mansion on Weston Hill about the same time.

Julie Perry was in the process of restoring the Bartlett mansion to its former grandeur. Before his accident, Tom Elliott had worked for nearly a year replacing rotten porches, reroofing it, and remodeling the outdated kitchen and bathrooms. Julie had selected sky blue paint for the outside of the house and white for shutters and gingerbread trim. A wide front door and downstairs windows had stained glass panels.

On the front lawn, Melissa and the children were playing a game of scrub ball. She waved. "Stop, Colby! Stop! We need another player."

He leaned his bicycle against a tree and strolled toward a small yellow and green bean bag that served as first base.

"Alan's up to bat, I'm pitching, and you and Annie will have to get him out." Melissa pushed a strand of blonde hair behind her ear. Then she faked a pinwheel windup, and slow-pitched the ball across the plate.

Whack! Alan slammed the ball directly to Colby, who tossed it gently to Annie, who put her brother out and became the next batter. Colby and Melissa played with the children until it was too dark to see the ball. Julie Perry came to the door and called, "Supper's ready, kids. Come in and wash up." Alan and Annie ran up the steps and into the house.

Melissa linked her arm through Colby's as they walked toward the porch. "Doc and Julie had a great time on the cruise," she said. "You should see their tans! And the kids were absolutely no trouble while they were gone, but I'm glad they're back. They brought us presents. See?" Melissa lifted her long blonde hair to reveal dangling earrings and a necklace made of shells, interwoven with coral beads and silver threads.

Colby bent his head to examine the intricate necklace. Suddenly, he was aware of Melissa's smooth, warm skin, and her lips, so close to his own. Embarrassed, he stepped back, thankful that dusk concealed the blush that covered his cheeks and ears.

"I'm glad Dr. Perry is back, Melissa," he stammered. "My dad needs an appointment with him real soon."

Melissa said, "Believe me, Colby, Dr. Perry is the best. If anything can be done for your dad, Doc's the man to do it. His new assistant Stan Sanders is great, too. He just graduated from college with a degree as a doctor's assistant. I think he's wonderful. He comes over to the house real often."

"My folks sure appreciated his house call."

"By the way, how is your dad?"

"Oh, much better, as far as the pain goes, but he still needs surgery if he's ever going to get out of that wheelchair."

"Bad things happen to us when we least expect it, Colby, but so do good things. Take my word for that."

"I hope you're right, Melissa! Well, I'd better hit the road. See you at school tomorrow."

"Say, Colby, I just remembered," and she reached for his hand. "On Saturday, December 18th, Doc and Julie are throwing a Christmas party. They're planning a fancy buffet, just like the one they had on the cruise ship. Pam usually helps me cook and serve, but she's going somewhere with her mom. Would you like to be my assistant and help prepare and serve the dinner?"

"Me? Gosh, Melissa, I don't know anything about that kind of stuff."

"Oh, it's easy. Julie has recipes. Just do what I tell you, and you'll soon be a first class chef."

"Well, I don't know. What will the Perrys say?"

"Oh, they always approve of anybody I say is okay. They'll pay you, too. Come on, Cole. Promise you'll help me."

"You're sure, now, that you can show me how to do all that fancy stuff."

"Cole, baby, I'll bet you can carry loaded trays of hors d'oeuvres and drinks balanced on one finger. Be here Saturday afternoon about 5:30, and I'll show you how to set the tables. By the way, what's your jacket size? I'll rent you a waiter's jacket with a cummerbund and bow tie to match my waitress outfit."

"Gosh. I don't know. The last jacket Mom bought me was a 38 long. But that was last year, and I've filled out since then. I guess a 40 long will be about right."

"You certainly have filled out," she said admiringly and patted his shoulders. "Do you have a pair of black dress slacks and a white shirt?"

"My church clothes will have to do." Standing so close to Melissa made Colby feel breathless and dizzy. Her eyes were green, flecked with brown, and tiny freckles dotted her nose and cheeks.

"Sounds perfect, Colby. You'll look wonderful. I'll talk to you again before band practice in the morning." She blew him a kiss as she climbed the steps and entered the house.

On the way home, Colby decided he was in love again. A month ago he'd been in love Linda, and now it was Melissa on his mind. He remembered dancing with her in the gym the night his tires were slashed, and how she'd helped ease his hurt feelings over Linda's "Dear Colby" letter. Melissa was responsible for taking care of the Perry's big home and their two children when they were away. She could even prepare and serve a buffet dinner for guests. Not only that, she was on the senior honor roll and played first chair clarinet in the band. What a girl!

    Compared to Melissa, Linda was just a spoiled brat. Sure, he remembered the gossip about Melissa that went around school after she came back from California. And he'd listened to Dalton's stories about Melissa in the locker room, but Dalton was a braggart and a liar.

    Melissa treated Colby like a grownup. Linda made him feel frustrated and jealous. Linda's fascination with Dalton's handsome face, his fancy car, and his Hollywood kisses were still sore spots, like emotional pimples beneath the surface of his skin. But those love bumps were healing fast. He hoped that Mr. Jenkins would recognize "Darling" Dalton as a conceited, beer guzzling phony and protect his vain and spoiled little girl.

    Meanwhile, Colby decided that being in love with Melissa was as exciting as white water rafting. Somehow, the urgency he'd felt for talking to Officer Reed about the marijuana cache sank like tiny pebbles to the bottom of his stream of consciousness.

CHAPTER THIRTEEN

The Saturday morning after Thanksgiving Day was cold but sunny, so Colby stuffed leftover turkey scraps into a plastic bag and rode his bicycle to Pickens' store. He intended to leave his bike and walk across the street to Weston Hill to inspect the pack rat's nest. If Lucky was running loose, they'd meet at the front gate and race on opposite sides of the fence toward the drug cache. Then they'd play fetch, and Colby would reward him with the meat scraps.

After he'd observed Mr. Pickens and Eddie entering the police station, Colby felt sure that Bert had blabbed the secret of the pack rat's nest to them. He felt betrayed, but Colby missed talking things over with Bert and hearing the latest school gossip. Bert was so quiet that the coaches often forgot he was in the office or locker room, so Bert knew the school scoop before anyone else did – stuff like who made the basketball team and whether the school might get a new gym.

As Colby entered Pickens' Store, Bert was placing sodas in the cooler. "Hey, Cole. Long time no see! What's happenin', man?" They exchanged high fives. No one else was in the store. "I'm headed over to Weston Hill. Want to check things out with me?"

"Can't. Soon as we close up at noon, we're headed to a tribal meeting at Burr Oak Springs. Wanna come? We're having a big feed and an all-night singing and stomp dance."

"Aw, your folks probably wouldn't like me butting in on your tribal stuff. Besides, I'm wearing my grubs, and you're all dressed up."

"No problem. Nobody else dresses up. Dad's the song leader and I'm supposed to play my guitar, so we have to look our best." Bert had plastered his straight black hair with gel. He had on a starched and ironed western shirt, new jeans, and a fancy leather belt with a silver buckle. The toes of his black Roper boots were polished to a high gloss.

"Sounds like a lot of fun, Bert, but I promised myself that I'd check out the pack rat's nest this morning to see if any rats have been nosing around. Maybe I'll get back to the store before you leave."

"Aw, Cole, what good will that do? Just get you in trouble. Leave it alone."

"Well, so far, that's exactly what I've done, and nothing's changed. I'll just run over to Weston Hill and be back in half an hour or so. Don't wait for me."

Colby jogged across Delmonte and headed down Weston Lane. Lucky was nowhere in sight. Squirrels and birds, foraging for nuts and seed paused momentarily to evaluate Colby's invasion of their domain. Then sensing no threat, they returned to the business of survival. The big black dog did not appear, so Colby left the pile of scraps at the gate.

He strolled down the path toward the log under which the marijuana cache was hidden. Suddenly, his eyes opened wide, and he began to run. Beneath the log was a gaping hole! Leaves and twigs were scattered, and the black plastic bag was gone. Someone had tossed beer cans into the empty cavity.

His thoughts swirled, and his ears roared from the pounding of his fast-beating heart. He felt sick enough to vomit. Now he was really in big trouble. By not reporting his discovery, he'd allowed drug dealers to sneak up and collect their stash. No matter what excuses he gave, he had become an accessory to a felony. He had allowed them to keep their loot hidden for nearly two months, and now they were probably selling it to potheads and gullible kids.

Colby wondered if the drug dealers knew that one bag was missing – the one he had taken. Feeling limber-legged, he walked slowly back to Pickens' store.

Mr. Pickens was locking the door to the pecan shed. Usually he had on rumpled khaki work clothes, but today, because he served as a tribal leader, he wore starched and ironed khaki pants with a quilted hunting vest and a white shirt. A braided leather bola with a turquoise clasp served as his necktie, and around his waist he wore a beaded belt with a silver belt buckle.

"Why, hello there, Colby." Mr. Pickens smoothed the wide brim of his black Stetson hat and creased the crown before replacing it on his head. "We're just leaving for a meeting at Burr Oak Springs. Want to come along?"

"Well, I – I'm not really dressed to go anywhere special."

"Aw, you look all right. Come inside the store and call your folks. Tell them you're going to a Chickasaw stomp dance with us. We won't get home until after midnight."

Colby did not know how to refuse Mr. Pickens' friendly invitation, so he said, "Well, if you're sure it's okay."

"Of course, it is," and Mr. Pickens slapped him on the back. Colby knew he should go to the police station and talk to Officer Reed right away, but he dreaded facing him. He had waited too long. Going to the Chickasaw celebration would just delay his confession. He hesitated.

"Colby's going with us, Bert," Mr. Pickens shouted, as they entered the store. Bert smiled broadly at Colby and made an AOK sign with his fingers. "While he's calling his folks, you run upstairs and bring down the folding chairs and the ice chest with the food and those sacks of Christmas goodies your mom fixed for the kids."

Mr. Pickens began emptying change from the cash register into a sack, which he placed inside a small safe in the floor. Then he turned off the electricity to the gasoline pumps. "Have to use extra precautions against thieves," he said, "especially when Officer Reed is off duty. He's a good friend of mine. He's gone to Texas for a couple of weeks to visit his wife's parents during the Christmas holiday."

Then he pointed a finger at Colby and said, "You need to have a talk with Officer Reed when he returns. He's a good listener."

Surprised by Mr. Pickens' remark, Colby nodded. Reed's holiday vacation had given him a reprieve. Silently he resolved to go to the police station the day after Christmas and tell Reed everything he knew, no matter what his punishment might be.

Bert called down the stairs, "Hey, Cole, help me carry this stuff to the car!" Mrs. Pickens had filled paper sacks with oranges, apples, nuts, and candies and tied each sack with a red bow. The boys carefully placed them in boxes and loaded them in the trunk of the car, along with chairs, an ice chest, and several containers of delicious-smelling food for the dinner.

Small and plump, Mrs. Pickens emerged carrying a huge cake. She smiled at Colby as he held the door open for her. Around her shoulders, she wore a fringed red shawl embroidered with flowers and leaves. "We're so pleased you are going with us," she said softly. Her brown eyes reminded Colby of rich, creamy chocolate.

Burr Oak Springs campground was located much farther away from Bartlett than Colby had imagined. In the car he had no opportunity to tell Bert that the marijuana packets were gone and that he'd messed up, big time. Reed's absence from Bartlett gave Colby a temporary reprieve, but anxiety and guilt hovered over him like dark clouds concealing a dangerous tornado funnel that was capable of destroying everything in its path.

CHAPTER FOURTEEN

As the car moved down the highway, Bert grinned and said, "You ever played stick ball, Cole?"

"Nope. What's it like? Tennis?"

"Yeah, kinda like that. But it's more like soccer. Here, I brought some extra sticks. See." And Bert reached into a sack and brought out two polished hickory sticks about two feet long with a pocket made of woven leather thongs attached to one end. Then he showed Colby a hard leather ball, the size of a big lemon.

"Back in the early days, tribes competed with each other with no limit on the number of players each team could have. Instead of fighting wars and losing men in battle, they played stick ball to win hunting rights or territory or even wives as the prize. Sometimes the entire tribe played – men, women, and children – just for fun."

Bert gently tossed the ball from one leather pocket to the other. "The action could get plenty rough, you know, just like those European soccer games you see on television, when the teams and fans go bananas and rough each other up. Dad says Native Americans taught the game to French explorers. They called it *baggataway*, but the French re-named it lacrosse because of the shape of the sticks."

"I've heard of lacrosse, but stick ball sounds like more fun. How do you Chickasaws play it?"

"Well, the object is to pick the ball up off the ground with your two sticks and hold it in that little pocket without touching the ball with your hands. A player can toss the ball from his leather pocket to a teammate's, but, believe me, the ball is really hard to catch."

"I can imagine!" said Colby.

"Then you have to run toward the goal post without losing the ball. Opponents are free to do whatever it takes to get the ball. It's rough, man. The other guys hack at you with their sticks. Sometimes players get bruised pretty bad trying to hang on to the ball. Then while you're holding the sticks like this, you have to toss the ball so that it flies out of the pocket and hits the goal post."

"You mean like chunking rocks at fence posts?"

"Yeah. Like that. We have a cow's skull fastened to our goal post as a target. I'll show you how to play when we get there. It's a rugged game, but you'll catch on fast. Girls can play if they want to, and some of them are really good at hitting the skull with the ball. The only thing is, boys aren't allowed to take the ball away from a girl. To me, that seems kinda unfair because most of the girls play rougher than the boys."

At last Mr. Pickens drove the car over a rickety wooden bridge that spanned a clear flowing creek and parked on dry grass beside other cars and pickups. In the middle of a clearing was a gigantic Burr Oak tree, at least fifty feet tall with branches as thick as telephone poles. The ground beneath it was covered with huge acorns. Colby could imagine the tree's dark green canopy of shady leaves during spring and summer. Now, most of the brown leaves had fallen. A lot of children had climbed the tree and were sitting on its bare branches, swinging their legs.

"Hey, Bert," one boy called. "Come play stick ball with us!"

"In a minute, dude, after I unload the car." Then Bert said, "Gimme a hand here, Cole, so we can hurry up and have some fun."

Mr. and Mrs. Pickens waved to friends and walked toward a barn-sized wooden building that had once been a school house. Wooden siding was covered with flaking white paint, and faded black letters over the doorway read BURR OAK SCHOOL. In front of the building was a well with a rope and pulley for the bucket. Two women were drawing water and pouring it into a pitcher.

At the side of the building stood the wooden frame of a brush arbor, thatched in winter with dead limbs and leaves. Bert explained that each spring tribal members cut fresh saplings and bushes for the arbor roof. "That brush arbor is where we hold open-air singings and church revivals in summer," said Bert.

Behind the building, Colby could see two privies marked Girls and Boys, and beyond that was a wide open field, where some of the Chickasaw boys and girls were playing a game that looked like stick ball.

Bert and Colby unloaded the ice chest, the folding chairs, blankets and pillows, boxes of Christmas sacks, and Bert's guitar case. Then they followed Mr. and Mrs. Pickens into the white building. Inside, adults and youths of all ages sat on benches along the walls talking and joking with one another.

With his curly auburn hair and fair and freckled skin, Colby had expected to stand out like a sore thumb at the tribal meeting. He imagined that all Chickasaws, like the Pickens family, would have straight black hair, brown skin, and brown eyes, but to his surprise, many did not fit this stereotype. Some had blonde hair, pale skins, and blue eyes. Several of the girls setting up tables were his classmates at Bartlett High. He had not realized that they were Chickasaws. He waved at Joni Worcester, a girl in his algebra class.

"Put the chest over there by the serving tables, Bert, and our chairs and blankets in the corner," said Mrs. Pickens. "The girls will take care of those Christmas sacks." Holding Bert by the arm, she said, "Don't forget to introduce Colby to everyone, and when your daddy rings the bell for assembly, wash up in the creek and come eat your dinner. Remember. You're on the program."

Bert and Colby ran across dead grass stubble behind the school house toward the stick ball field, where Bert's cousin Eddie and about fifteen other teenagers were playing stickball.

"Here are your sticks, Cole," said Bert. "You be on Eddie's team, and I'll be on Franklin's. He's that guy over there with his hair in braids."

Colby wondered how he'd recognize which players were his teammates, but it really didn't matter because he never got a chance to snare the ball in his leather pouch. Other players were so skillful and quick that he found himself running up and down the field, never gaining possession of the ball once. Eddie and Franklin were the best players, but Franklin's team won.

"Sorry, Eddie, that I didn't play better," said Colby.

"No problem, man. Stick ball takes practice. Come and play with us again."

Soon the big bell signaled that the meal was ready, so the stick ball players washed up in the creek and hurried to the white building. Mr. Pickens stood at the front of the room, and everyone else formed a circle at the perimeter. Then in the Chickasaw language, Mr. Pickens led tribal members in a song. Colby could not understand the words, but he knew it was a prayer of thanksgiving.

He had never tasted such delicious food. Fried chicken, corn bread, pashofa, fry bread, corn, chili and beans, cole slaw, peach pickles, sweet potatoes, turkey and dressing, chocolate cake, and apricot fried pies.

After the feast, Mr. Pickens conducted a brief business meeting. The tribe discussed buying a van to transport elderly members to the new hospital and voted money for upkeep on campground facilities. A woman brought up the problem of drug and alcohol abuse among youth in the tribe. Mr. Pickens explained that leaders were exploring solutions. Several families announced weddings and new babies, and someone read a list of those who were sick and unable to come. They discussed the upcoming Red Earth Festival, when Native American tribes from North America would meet in Oklahoma City for a gigantic stomp dance at the Civic Center.

Mr. Pickens said, "As you know, other tribes at the festival will compete in the native dances, especially the Plains Tribes. They always have elaborate costumes and win all the prizes. Oklahoma Chickasaws never have competed much, but Joni and Franklin have studied a videotape prepared by the Eastern Chickasaws, who live in Mississippi. Later today, they'll demonstrate the way our people danced before removal of the Civilized Tribes to Oklahoma. Now I want everyone, especially the youngsters, to participate."

Bert and Eddie were elected tribal "clowns," which meant they would march in the opening procession. Bert whispered, "It's a tradition. We're supposed to wear costumes and paint our faces and act crazy to see if we can make the solemn and dignified tribal elders laugh."

Then Mr. Pickens introduced Bert, who tuned his guitar and led tribal members in familiar hymns. When Bert began to sing in the Chickasaw language, Colby was surprised. Not only could Bert sing well, he could sing in two languages. The Chickasaws had fine voices. When they sang "Amazing Grace," Colby sang along in English.

Shilombish Holitopa ma!
Ish minti pulla cha,
Hatak ilbusha pia ha
Ish pi yukpalashke.

Mr. Pickens then preached a sermon about the meaning of the coming Christmas season and how people should celebrate the birth of Jesus with new beginnings and hope. "Even though nature seems cold and dead in December," he said, "seeds and roots of renewal are in the ground, just as faith and hope and love are in our hearts, ready to be reborn."

After the meeting was over, teenage girls distributed Christmas sacks to every child in the room. Mrs. Pickens had prepared enough for the big kids, too, even Colby and Bert.

At dusk, Eddie and Franklin lit a bonfire outside, and everyone sat on blankets or low chairs in a circle around it. Colby sat by himself on a blanket at the edge of the circle. It was the first time he had felt excluded from tribal activities. The day had been so pleasant and full of excitement, he'd almost forgotten about the pack rat's nest and the confession he'd have to make to Officer Reed.

In the shadows beyond the smoke and flames of the fire, Colby saw Eddie talking to Franklin. Their heads were bent close together, as though they shared a secret. They glanced toward him, but when they saw that he was watching them, Franklin frowned, and they turned their backs. Colby wondered if they were talking about him. Then he saw Eddie hand Franklin a small packet, which he quickly shoved into his jacket pocket. What was in that packet? Marijuana? Eddie and Franklin? Potheads? Dealers? No way! They were Chickasaw youth leaders. Colby reassured himself that the packet was probably just a plug of chewing tobacco or an extra slice of Mrs. Pickens' cake.

At the bonfire, Mr. Pickens signaled the start of dancing. He and several tribal elders took turns beating on a large kettle drum. It was made out of an iron barrel cut in half with a tanned cow hide stretched tightly across it. Drum sticks were made of bois d'arc wood with leather balls on the ends. In rhythm with drum beats, the elders chanted something that sounded to Colby like "Hah yah! Hah yah! Hah yah! Hah yah."

Soon the young men fell into line behind Franklin and began dancing around the fire. Each man performed intricate steps and circular movements to the rhythm of the pounding drums. Colby thought Bert and Eddie were the best.

When Joni led the women and girls around the fire, she held her body very straight while her feet shuffled sideways. The women opened their shawls like birds' wings and slowly glided around the circle. Colby could see colorful embroidery on the backs of their shawls.

For a while the stomp dancing fascinated Colby, but soon the flickering firelight, a full stomach, the swaying movements of the dancers and the rhythm of the drum lulled him to sleep. It was nearly dawn when Bert shook him awake. "Hey, Cole. The party's over. Time to load up."

During the drive home, Mr. and Mrs. Pickens were silent. Colby wanted to ask Bert who Franklin was, but Bert was sound asleep. When they reached the store, it was dawn – time for Colby to throw his Sunday morning paper route. He helped Bert and Mr. Pickens unload the car and thanked them.

Then he rode his bicycle downtown to the *Bartlett Banner*, where a stack of Sunday editions awaited him on the loading dock. A bold headline read:

ILLEGAL DRUGS SUSPECTED IN FATAL CAR CRASH

The story said the crash had killed one man and injured two others. The police had found marijuana and drug paraphernalia inside the car. A wave of guilt swept over Colby as he read the story. The identity of the mangled driver was no one Colby knew, but he realized that if he had told Officer Reed about the drug cache, perhaps the accident would not have occurred, and the drug dealers would be in jail.

CHAPTER FIFTEEN

Old-timers say if you don't like the weather in Oklahoma, wait a minute. Sunshine and mild temperatures can change overnight if an arctic wind comes sweeping down the plains across Nebraska and Kansas. When Colby awoke, his room was dark. The electric clock on his bedside table flashed 2:10, but his wristwatch said 4:30. Jeanie appeared in the doorway carrying a kerosene lantern they used on camping trips.

"The power is off, Colby. Electric lines are down all over town. School's been canceled because of icy roads and the power outage, but the hospital never shuts down. The engineer just activates the auxiliary generator. I have to be at work in thirty minutes." Colby sat up and looked outside. A coating of ice crystals etched window panes on the north side of the house.

"Get dressed in some warm clothes because you'll have to fasten chains on the tires for me. Tom's awake. He'll tell you how to do it while I finish dressing."

Colby arose from a warm nest of blankets and shivered as he searched in a drawer for long underwear and a flannel shirt. Without electricity, temperature inside the house had dropped to near-freezing. He pulled on jeans and heavy socks and reached for his boots.

The plastic bag of green marijuana leaves lay untouched in the toe of the left boot. Gosh! It had been nearly two months since his discovery. He quickly shoved the bag between the mattress and box springs and pulled on his boots. Then he grabbed a stocking cap and gloves from a drawer and removed his heavy jacket from a hook behind the door.

Jeanie had covered Tom with extra blankets and a crocheted afghan. He wore a bright orange stocking cap and mittens, which he usually wore during hunting season. Colby cranked up the head of his hospital bed so they could talk.

"You look like Santa Claus in his sleigh, Dad," he said.

"On a morning like this, I don't feel like doing the Ho! Ho! Ho! Thing. When my ears are cold, I'm cold all over. This weather's not fit for man or beast, but your mom insists that she's going to work anyway. Hospital patients need their food, bad weather or not, and she's already missed several days of work taking care of me. I'm afraid, Colby, we'd have to lie in front of the wheels of the pickup to stop her, so let's do what we can to make driving on icy streets as safe as possible."

Then Tom gave Colby directions for attaching chains to the tires. "If you have any problems, bring one of the chains in here to the bed and I'll show you. What's the temp? Seems like it must be thirty below zero."

"I don't know, Dad, but I'll turn on the car radio and get a weather report while I'm out in the garage."

Ice-glazed bushes in the yard looked like crystal figurines, and limbs on trees lining the street had broken under the weight of the ice. A strong north wind made the limbs tinkle like wind chimes. Weeds and tall grass in a nearby vacant lot looked like hundreds of bent wires encased in glass, and icicles hanging from electric lines made them sag dangerously low between poles so they nearly touched the ground.

He opened the garage doors and stepped inside, where he was protected from a blast of the frigid north wind. He inserted a key in the ignition of the pickup and tried to start it, but the engine was cold. Just as he was about to give up, the engine fired. He left the pickup running, turned on the heater, and tuned the radio to a country-western station. The weatherman said the temperature was 20 degrees with a wind chill factor of minus 10 degrees.

Tire chains hung from a peg in a corner of the garage. There's a first time for everything, he thought as he began attaching chains to the tires. After he checked each chain to make sure it was fastened, he entered the kitchen and called, "Car's ready, Mom."

Buttoning her red coat with the parka and then pulling on a pair of fuzzy black gloves, Jeanie emerged from the bedroom. "Colby, honey, how can I ever thank you enough?"

"Dad and I wish you wouldn't try to go in to work, Mom. The streets are slick as glass. Can't you take the day off? Others probably will."

"That's just the reason I must go. When I called the supervisor, she said they are short-handed. Since you are out of school today, you can stay with your dad and prepare his meals. I'll be home in time for you to throw your papers. You may have to walk your route today."

"Maybe the sun will shine and warm things up. Now remember, Mom. Some drivers won't have chains on their tires, so look out for them and drive slowly. When you get to the hospital, call us so we'll know you're okay."

"My goodness, Colby, you sound just like your father. But I will be careful." She rumpled his hair. "Why don't you build a fire in the fireplace? Otherwise, Tom will have to spend the day in bed. The wood is wet, but maybe you can get it started. If the electricity doesn't come on soon, you can use the camp stove to cook breakfast. Set it on top of the stove so you don't burn the cabinet top."

"We'll be fine, Mom. Don't worry about us. Take care of yourself and come home safe."

After Jeanie left, Colby walked to the woodpile behind the house and brought in an armload of wood. The Elliotts seldom used their fireplace during cold weather because emptying the ashes was such a hassle, and any warmth from the house escaped right up the chimney instead of heating the room. Before his accident, Tom loved to build a fire on cool, rainy fall days and watch football games on television. Colby used a stack of old newspapers and finally coaxed wet logs to burn. Soon a cozy fire was blazing. He found his dad's warm clothes and helped him dress.

"I wonder what folks would think if they came calling, and found me sitting here in my camouflage suit and orange hunting cap?" Tom laughed as Colby pushed the wheelchair into the living room close to the glowing fire.

He set up the propane camp stove and cooked a hearty hunter's breakfast. First he fried bacon, and as it sizzled in the pan, he stirred pancake batter and made a pot of boiled coffee. When the stack was piled ten pancakes high, he scrambled eggs and served breakfast on television trays in front of the fire.

In spite of the inconvenience from the ice storm, they were as content as hunters beside a campfire in the deer woods. After breakfast, Tom taught Colby how to play pinochle, and they passed the morning playing cards in intense competition.

Occasionally, Colby arose to throw on another log or to stir the pot of pinto beans cooking on the camp stove or to wash some potatoes, which he wrapped in foil and laid in coals at the edge of the fireplace.

He wanted to tell his dad about the marijuana cache on Weston Hill, but hesitated. He wished Tom was strong enough to go with him to the police station for a talk with Officer Reed, but the man who sat in front of the fire had enough worries, so Colby remained silent.

At noon he put new batteries in the portable radio and once again, they were in contact with the outside world. The weatherman predicted cold and more snow on top of the ice. After lunch, Colby stoked the fire and carefully placed the screen in front of it. Then he helped his dad back to bed and piled on another blanket.

"Will you be okay while I throw my papers?"

"Sure. I'll be fine. I'll read for a few minutes and probably take a nap. Your mom should be home soon. Be extra careful out on the street. People aren't used to driving on ice, so stay on the sidewalk when you can."

Colby dressed in his warmest clothes, and because he did not own a pair of rubber boots, he placed plastic garbage bags over each cowboy boot and fastened the tops with rubber bands.

"You look like the abominable snowman, Cole," said Tom. "Watch out for traffic."

Colby pedaled to the Banner, where he sat in the shelter of the loading dock and began rolling and stuffing papers into plastic sleeves. None of the carriers had shown up, so Mr. Kennedy was loading papers into his pickup that had chains on the tires.

"Thanks for coming in, Colby. You should get a bonus for being such a dependable employee. Tell you what, if you'll throw the papers for me from the passenger side, I'll drive, and we'll get your route and the other routes done a lot faster. You'll be inside the truck instead of out in the cold on that bike."

Mr. Kennedy drove slowly up and down the streets of Bartlett. Other motorists' cars had slid off the roads and were abandoned. When Colby threw the Banner on porches or driveways, people rushed outside to retrieve it, as if isolation made them crave news from the outside world.

Mr. Kennedy asked, "How are your folks, Colby?"

"Oh, Dad's a little bit better. He's taking some new medicine to ease his pain, but he still needs surgery. We're just waiting to see what Dr. Perry recommends." And until money falls from heaven, he thought.

He started to tell Mr. Kennedy about the marijuana stash and to ask his advice, but before he could gather courage to say anything, they were back at the Banner building.

"Put your bike in the truck, Colby, and I'll take you home. It's starting to snow again, and the temperature has dropped. I'm going your way anyhow – just be a minute. I have to run inside to get Mary. She helped me get the paper out today."

Mary and Mr. Kennedy emerged from the office. Dressed in a white ski outfit, she reminded Colby of a fluffy marshmallow. In English class, when Mary leaned forward to tell him the latest joke, her green eyes, fringed with reddish brown lashes, made him think of sparkling water and deep forests. She could make the dullest poem or book sound interesting. He leaped out of the pickup to hold the door for her.

"Hi, Cole," she said and climbed inside the cab. "What's happenin'?"

"Not much. I didn't know you worked at the paper."

"If you had ever come inside the Banner office, you'd know it. I'm there, like, every afternoon after school. Dad operates the Banner on a shoestring, so he does lots of interviews and on-the-scene reports, and if he doesn't have time to finish a story, I use his notes and write it for him on the computer."

Mr. Kennedy asked Mary, "Did Elvin get pictures of that wreck over on Elm Street?"

"Yep, he was getting ready to scan it into tomorrow's edition when we left. We had lots of calls this morning asking when the electricity would come back on. Residential areas still don't have any power. With all of the frozen pipes and other stuff, we should get some good human interest stories out of this."

Colby was impressed. Mary was a reporter!

"Say, Cole, have you finished reading *Great Expectations*?" she asked.

"Almost. What did you think of it?"

"Oh, it was okay, but Pip and his true love Estella are such nerds. Imagine! Pip spending his inheritance trying to become a gentleman, whatever that is, and Estella marrying someone she doesn't even love, just because he's rich. Have you seen the movie yet?"

"No. We don't have a DVD player."

"You don't? Gosh, come over and we'll watch some films together. Mrs. McPherson said she'd give us bonus points if we'd watch *A Christmas Carol* and write a character sketch about Ebenezer Scrooge."

"Who's he?"

"For heaven's sake, Colby! He's the Bah! Humbug! character in Dickens' story. He's the miser that hates Christmas until three ghosts visit him and give him an attitude adjustment."

"Well, I haven't even finished reading *Great Expectations*."

"Procrastination won't get you anywhere fast, Colby."

How true, he thought. I keep putting off doing my school work and talking to Officer Reed and...

The pickup stopped at his street and Mr. Kennedy said, "Here's your corner, Colby. Thanks again for coming in. I'll see you tomorrow, and we'll do the same thing if the weather's still bad."

Colby climbed out and lifted his bicycle from the bed of the truck onto the pavement. He waved at Mr. Kennedy and Mary as they drove off. When he entered the house, the phone was ringing. It was Jeanie calling from the hospital. "Lots of people couldn't make it to work, so I'm staying for another shift. I think I'll just spend the night here in one of the lounges instead of trying to come home. That way I'll be here for the morning shift, too. Are you getting along all right?"

"Sure thing. The electricity hasn't come on yet, but we're warm. Dad's okay. Don't worry, Mom. We'll be fine," he said and replaced the receiver.

After supper, Tom read the paper and went to bed early. Colby sat in front of the fire, and by the light of the kerosene lantern finished reading *Great Expectations*. He closed the book, and as he gazed into the glowing embers, he recalled the many unusual characters in Dickens' novel.

Those Victorians were not so different from people in Bartlett, he reasoned. Linda is something like Estella, and Miss Weston is a mysterious old recluse, like Miss Havisham. Satis House is like the Weston mansion, built of stone and surrounded by an iron fence.

He wondered what tragedy had twisted Miss Weston's life. Had she really murdered her father and sister? Naw, he decided. She can't be the Lizzie Borden of Bartlett like people say she is. Maybe her boyfriend dumped her on their wedding day, like Miss Havisham's lover did. That's a possibility, but it's a sure bet Miss Weston doesn't wear a tattered old wedding gown like Miss Havisham. The time I saw her, he thought, she had on black, like a witch. But a witch wouldn't have a neat pet like Lucky. Oh, he's her guard dog all right. Just a word from her turns him into a killer, but I'll bet she pets him and gives him lots of affection. He probably sleeps at the foot of her bed.

As he banked the fire with a large, slow-burning log and placed the fire screen in front of it, he wondered if Miss Weston and Lucky were safe and warm during the ice storm. He wondered if Miss Weston ever celebrated Christmas. Probably not. How could you sing carols and exchange presents with a dog? Even one as nice as Lucky.

CHAPTER SIXTEEN

Sunshine soon melted the snow and ice, and Bartlett returned to traditional pre-Christmas activities. Colby threw his papers quickly in order to arrive at the Perry's house in time to help Melissa with the party.

As he rode his bicycle through the melting slush, he waved to some people who were constructing a manger scene in front of the Baptist church. City workers on ladders were draping silver garlands and lights on Main Street. He pedaled up the brick-paved driveway of the Perry's Victorian mansion and entered the back door.

"Am I ever glad to see you!" exclaimed Melissa, who was spreading soft cheese on circles of rye bread and placing a sliced green olive with a red pimiento in the center of each one. She wore a white canvas apron splattered with ketchup, mustard, chocolate, and other food stains.

"With a few tinsel garlands and a gold star on your head, you could pass for a Christmas tree," Colby said.

"Nuff said, joker. We've got lots and lots to do before party time." Wiping her hands on her apron, she said, "Here. Take a look at this list."

Colby scanned a long list that began with "decorate porch, entry hall, stairs, and table" and ended with "slice turkey and ham and arrange on platter."

"Why don't you take care of those decorations while I finish these hors d'oeuvres."

"You mean you're not going to show me how to do this stuff?"

"No. Be creative. Whatever you do will be okay. Just take the kids' junk to the back yard and sweep off the front porch. Julie left a box of decorations in the hall – some votive candles to outline the front walk and colored lights and garlands and the usual Christmas stuff."

Melissa licked the spoon and washed her hands. Then she covered the tray of sandwiches with plastic wrap. She placed the tray in the refrigerator and began to pat a mixture of raw hamburger meat and spices into small meatballs, which she arranged on a cookie sheet and shoved into the oven.

"Time's a-wastin', Cole. Get with it!"

Colby loaded toys on the porch into a red wagon and pulled it around back. Then he found the broom and swept the porch, the steps, and front walk. With the broom handle, he demolished what was left of a melting snowman. Then he dragged the box of decorations onto the porch. He placed eighteen red votive candles inside milk glass containers with metal holders and tied them with red and green bows. He pushed them into soft dirt at three foot intervals along both sides of the walk. Before the guests' arrival at dusk, he'd light the candles.

The Perrys had not put up a Christmas tree yet so they would have more room for their guests, but a florist had delivered a huge pine cone wreath for the front door, and poinsettias dressed in shiny red and green paper for the tables and buffet. Colby draped garlands of silver and red tinsel on the Victorian hall tree and stair balustrade. On the mantle, he found a fresh sprig of mistletoe with lots of white berries wrapped in green florist paper, and he hung it in the center of the door frame between the wide hall and parlor.

Then he reported to Melissa, who was arranging deviled eggs on a platter. "Job's done, chef. What's next?"

"Wash your hands and take a break. I need a gourmet to check my cuisine."

"A who to do what?" said Colby.

Melissa laughed. "An expert to taste the food, dummy. You look hungry, and after the crowd gets here, we won't have time to breathe, much less sample the food."

Melissa prepared Colby a plate with a spoonful of each dish she had prepared for the buffet. Swedish meatballs, shrimp salad, cinnamon apples, raw vegetables and spinach dip, tiny biscuits, sliced turkey and ham, and deviled eggs.

"Gosh, Mel, this is the best food I ever ate. You're a wonderful cook! Where'd you learn to fix chow like this?"

"I can read, Colby. Cookbooks of Julie's. Believe me, I've made some messes, but the Perrys never complain. Haven't you heard that old line about the way to get a husband is through his stomach? Well, I'm planning to get one. He's on my Christmas wish list."

"If I was old enough, I'd marry you in a minute, Melissa."

"Thanks for the offer, Colby. That's sweet. But now! Ta Da! A sample of desserts on the menu: pecan pie, cheesecake, or chocolate mousse."

"Gosh, Mel, I'm stuffed. Couldn't you put a plate aside for me to eat later? How about a sample of all three?"

"Sure thing. But we've got to hurry! First we'll set the table, fill the punch bowl, and then dress in our waiter and waitress outfits. They're hanging in the closet. When the guests begin to arrive, you answer the door and hang their coats in the closet or lay them on the bed in the downstairs bedroom. After Julie and Michael invite everybody to the buffet, you come into the kitchen and help me. We'll put more food out and gather up the dirty dishes on these trays."

"Gosh, what if I drop one and break those fancy glasses?"

"Colby, with your athletic ability, you could balance a tray on your nose." Melissa looked up at the kitchen clock. "It's nearly time for Michael and Julie to come home and dress. They'll probably have some last minute instructions for us. The kids are spending the night with friends, so I don't have to worry about them."

She showed Colby how to place china plates, napkins, silverware, and trays of food on the buffet and dining table. She made a quick survey of the parlor and told him to set up some folding chairs. Outside he lit the votive candles, which glowed a warm red, and the house and food were ready for the party to begin.

Colby and Melissa dressed themselves in elegant, rented costumes. Melissa wore a maid's short, black uniform with a ruffled white apron and frilly cap and black hose and heels that accentuated her slim ankles and shapely legs. Colby wore a tuxedo and cummerbund with a white ruffled shirt and black satin bow tie. The outfit even included white gloves.

Standing side-by-side in the front hall under the mistletoe, they admired themselves in the full length gilt-framed Victorian mirror. "Don't we look great?" said Melissa. "I'll bet some of the guests will think we're brother and sister."

Dazzled by the elaborate decorations, the food, and Melissa's beauty, Colby said, "You're prettier than any sister I could ever imagine, Melissa." And just as Colby put his arm around Melissa's waist and turned to kiss her, Dr. Perry called out from the doorway, "Hey, Mel. Where's the punch?"

"Oh gosh, I forgot!" said Melissa, and she hurried into the kitchen.

Julie Perry smiled at Colby as she climbed the stairs to dress. "House looks nice," she murmured.

Dr. Perry extended his hand toward Colby. "Michael Perry," he said as they shook. "You and Melissa look enough alike to be brother and sister. Are you a long-lost cousin?"

"No. I'm Colby Elliott. You're my dad's doctor."

"Why, of course. When Mel told me she'd invited you to help her tonight with the party, I didn't make the connection. How is Tom?"

"Not so good. While you were on vacation, he had a bad spell. Your assistant Steve Sanders came to the house and gave him some medicine."

"I haven't had time to look over Steve's reports, but Tom probably needs to come into the office for a check-up tomorrow."

Melissa returned with two bottles of sparkling white grape juice, which she poured into a crystal punch bowl over red and green maraschino cherries. Then into a silver bowl she poured a pitcher of rich, creamy eggnog and sprinkled nutmeg on top.

The doorbell rang. "Wow! Company's here already. I've got to run upstairs and dress," said Dr. Perry. "Talk to you later."

In the movies, butlers always bow and announce the guests' names, but Colby just grinned and said, "Merry Christmas" as he took their wraps. He knew some of the adults, like Steve Sanders and Mr. and Mrs. Kennedy.

"My goodness, Colby," said the Banner publisher. "You look like a movie star in that tuxedo."

Being a butler was fun until Colby saw Mr. and Mrs. Pembroke coming across the porch. He wondered if Principal Pembroke would connect him with Officer Reed and the drug dog and his "forgotten" conference with the school counselor.

Just as the Pembrokes stepped inside the door and Colby reached for their coats, the Perrys came downstairs. Mr. Pembroke stepped forward to shake hands with the host and hostess and never even looked at Colby. Laughter and conversation in the parlor intensified, and Colby happily faded into the background.

Throughout the evening as he replaced platters of food on the buffet table, Colby was careful to keep his back turned toward Mr. Pembroke. Soon guests gathered around Julie at the piano and sang Christmas songs, while Melissa and Colby cleared away the dishes.

They removed the leaves from the dining table and placed it against the wall so that the floor was open for dancing. From the kitchen Melissa and Colby could hear feet shuffling across the polished hardwood floor to the music of Dr. Perry's "golden oldie" CDs. They loaded the dishwasher, and Melissa washed, as Colby dried the crystal and silver.

When a country western song, "Blue Christmas," wafted through the kitchen door, Colby said, "How about a dance, Mel?" She smiled and melted into his arms. Colby closed his eyes as they slow danced around the kitchen. This has to be true love, he thought.

Suddenly the door swung open, and Steve Sanders stood there holding a sprig of mistletoe. "Hey, baby, great dinner. You are without a doubt the best cook in the world." To Colby he said, "How about me cutting in for a dance with my girl, kid?"

Melissa whirled away from Colby and threw herself into Steve's arms. He laughed as he held the mistletoe over her head and kissed her. Wrapped tightly in each other's arms, they danced around the kitchen. Colby's heart plummeted.

Still holding Steve's hand, Melissa turned to Colby and said, "We haven't told a soul yet, not even Julie and Michael, but we are getting married as soon as I graduate in May. You are the very first to know."

Colby stammered, "Well, congratulations. I'm real surprised and glad for you." Red-faced and embarrassed, he wanted to vanish. "If you don't have any more jobs for me, Mel, I – I think I'll run along. I have to get up early in the morning."

"Well, sure, Colby. You were a wonderful butler tonight. Next time the Perrys give a party, I'll ask you to help me again. I kind of liked being your big sister. We make a good team."

Colby went into the bathroom and changed into his jeans and knit shirt. He hung the rented tuxedo up carefully on a hanger and pulled on his jacket. When he emerged, Melissa and Steve were smooching by the refrigerator. He cleared his throat.

"Merry Christmas," he said to Melissa, and he shook hands with Steve.

"Hey, wait a minute, Cole. Dr. Perry said to give you this check."

Colby glanced at the amount. Fifty dollars! "That can't be right, Melissa. It's too much."

"Dr. Perry thinks you did a great job. Take it and buy Christmas presents with it. Now you be careful going home. It's late." Melissa blew him a kiss as he closed the door.

As he pedaled his bicycle home, Colby softly hummed the melody to "Blue Christmas" and vowed never to fall in love again. The ice storm and Melissa and the Perry's party had pushed facing Officer Reed to the back of his mind. His scheme to catch the drug dealers had been a failure. The ice storm had put a stop to Colby's surveillance from the pecan tree, and the drug dealers had come for the contents of the black plastic bag when he was not even around, just as Bert had predicted.

Officer Reed would return from Texas in a few more days. He'd have to confess, but he doubted that Reed would believe his story. He dreaded the effect his actions would have on his parents. He hoped it wasn't too late for Reed to catch whoever had removed the packets of marijuana from the pack rat's nest.

CHAPTER SEVENTEEN

Jeanie left decorating the Christmas tree up to Colby, so he cut a small cedar tree growing on Weston Road and decorated it with baubles and lights. They blinked a friendly greeting from the window each evening when he returned home at dusk.

With money from his job as the Perrys' waiter, Colby had bought Jeanie a blue sweater and Tom a book on fly fishing wrapped up in red tissue paper. On Christmas morning they exchanged presents. Colby grinned when he opened his small package and discovered a mobile telephone.

"Oh, wow! This is wonderful! But these phones cost a lot of money."

Tom said, "Don't worry about it, son. Being able to contact you in case of emergency was more important to us than our gold wedding bands. The subscription is paid for a year." He smiled at Jeanie. "Now your mother can quit worrying about you when you are late coming home."

Colby read the directions and punched in their home phone number. When the phone rang Tom answered and said, "Ho! Ho! Ho! Merry Christmas."

Jeanie went into the kitchen to set the table. Rather than preparing dinner at home, she had brought three trays of turkey, dressing, green beans, sweet potatoes, cranberry gelatin, hot rolls, gravy, and pumpkin pie from the hospital.

In past years, she and Tom had sung special Christmas music in the church choir and carried food baskets to families less fortunate than theirs. Now Tom's disability and constant pain hung like a gray cloud over the heads of the Elliott family.

After dinner, Colby rode his bike to Weston Hill with his new mobile phone and turkey scraps for Lucky in his pocket. As he pedaled slowly down Delmonte, he remembered what Mr. Pickens had said about Christmas, that it was a time to celebrate new beginnings in life. Tomorrow, he would tell Officer Reed what he knew about the pack rat's nest and take his punishment.

He did not stop to talk to Bert but turned into Weston Lane. In the distance through trees, now bare of leaves, he could see the limestone mansion, white as a skull. Not a puff of smoke arose from the chimney. He wondered what Miss Weston might be doing on Christmas Day.

To his surprise, the wrought iron gate stood wide open on rusty hinges. A car had passed through it recently. Tire tracks had left black marks on wet leaves that covered the brick paving. Even in dazzling sunshine, the path leading to the mansion looked lonely and forbidding. Except for caws of a few crows and fluttering blue jays, everything was silent. Colby felt his heart begin to pound. His first impulse was to return quickly to the familiar streets of Bartlett, where people were celebrating Christmas.

Instead, he leaned his bicycle against one of the stone pillars and followed the tire tracks. Dusty cedars lining the driveway formed a dark green tunnel. Many limbs were broken, as if the car had forced its way through the narrow driveway at great speed. The turpentine smell of resin and dust made him sneeze, and he recalled the Halloween prank he'd played with Bert and Skeeter.

To his disappointment, there was no sign of Lucky. Colby wondered if the dog would attack him if Miss Weston gave the command. He hadn't forgotten her shotgun blast, but curiosity about the car overcame his fear. Maybe she has relatives that nobody knows about, he thought. Or maybe some people from the church have brought her a Christmas basket.

Emerging from the driveway, he was surprised to see Dalton Barrett's black Corvette parked under the carport at the side of the house, but the mansion's windows, like closed eyes, were tightly shuttered. Stealthily, he crossed the weed-choked parkway and climbed the broad stone steps of the verandah. He started to raise the heavy lion's head knocker on the front door, but loud, angry voices and Lucky's frantic barking from somewhere inside the mansion stopped him.

Impulsively, he crossed the verandah to the carport. On the back seat of the Corvette, he could see a plastic bag of marijuana and empty beer cans. Peering through a leaded glass pane on the side door, he could see overturned chairs, broken vases, and statues littering a faded red carpet. The door was open, just a crack, so Colby stepped inside.

"Where's the safe hidden, you old witch?" shouted a voice from the large room at the end of a long hallway.

"Please! Please! You're hurting me. I've told you over and over. All the money I have in the house is in my purse."

"Twenty measly bucks! Who do you think you're kidding? We know you've got lots of money and jewelry stashed around here someplace."

"Please. Don't hurt me anymore! Take the silver and paintings! They're all very valuable. I'll write you a check and never tell a soul that you were here!"

"That junk is worthless, and nobody in Bartlett would cash your check. Twist her arm again, Travis. Make her talk."

Miss Weston groaned, and Lucky began barking with renewed fury. Colby reasoned that Travis and Dalton had somehow overpowered Lucky and shut him up in a room near the side door, probably the kitchen. To rescue Miss Weston, Colby knew he had to think and act fast.

Backing silently out of the side door Colby reached into his pocket for his mobile phone and punched in 911.

"This is the emergency operator. How may I help you?"

"Call the police and send an ambulance to Weston Hill! They'll kill old lady Weston if you don't get here fast."

"May I have your name and address and the nature of the emergency, please?"

"No time now for all that stuff! Weston Hill on Delmonte Drive. For God's sake, hurry!"

"Be calm, sir. We have to confirm that this is not a prank call. Now what is your name again? Are you a resident at that address?"

"No. I'm Colby Elliott. Send help to Weston Hill. Delmonte Drive. Call Officer Reed! Call Mr. Pickens! Call Dr. Perry! Just get help!"

Colby closed the phone and stuffed it into his pocket. He didn't know whether to scream or cry in frustration. Instead, he took a deep breath and quietly entered the house. It's up to me, he thought.

He stood transfixed in the doorway. Sunshine was warm on his back, but in front of him lay the cold, musty interior of the house. Dad's remark, that no one who entered Weston Mansion ever returned to tell of it, flashed through his mind.

Gathering courage, he cautiously moved forward. From the room at the end of the hall he could hear glass breaking and upholstery being ripped. Lucky continued to bark. He was penned up inside the kitchen, only a few doors away. As Colby tiptoed past a majestic grandfather's clock in the hallway, his heart beat in rhythm with the pendulum's ominous tick-tock.

"She's done passed out," said Travis.

"Keep searching," said Dalton. "The old woman's got to have lots of dough hid out someplace."

Colby crept down the hallway, careful not to trip on broken furniture or shards of glass. He was uncertain what Lucky would do if he released him. The big dog might attack him instead of Dalton and Travis. Colby knew he had to take a chance because Lucky was the only backup he had.

As he slowly turned the knob to the kitchen where Lucky was penned, the dog clawed frantically at the door's wooden panels. Colby flung wide the door and jumped behind it as Lucky lunged into the hall, ready to kill. With ears flattened against his skull, his white fangs bared, and muscles steeled to attack, he raced toward the attackers.

Travis and Dalton were pulling books from shelves, searching for hidden loot with their backs turned. The angry dog hit Dalton like a cannonball between his shoulders and knocked him down. Then he tore at the back of Dalton's thick neck, sinking his fangs deep into the flesh. Dalton screamed and twisted, trying to protect his face and ears from the ferocious dog's razor sharp teeth.

Travis turned like a coward and headed for the door, but Colby blocked his escape. He tackled Travis, and they rolled across the rubble-strewn room, punching, and clawing each other. Although Travis was the larger of the two, Colby's fury gave him extra strength. Pot smoking and beer drinking had weakened Travis, and soon his movements grew sluggish. Blood and mucous smeared his nose and mouth, and he began to gasp for breath.

Colby dragged Travis to his feet and shoved him toward a corner of the room, where Lucky stood growling over Dalton's body. "Sit over in that corner with your back against the wall and don't move!" Lucky paced in front of the two partners in crime, guarding them and growling as if daring them to try an escape. Dalton's handsome face was ravaged and torn. He mumbled incoherently as if he might be in shock.

Colby wiped his own bloody nose on a piece of torn drapery and breathed deeply. Then he untied Miss Weston and gently lowered her limp and unconscious body to the floor. She's dead, he thought. He shuddered as he knelt beside her and felt for a pulse in her thin wrist. Miss Weston opened her eyes and groaned. "Thank God, you've come," she whispered.

Colby thrust a pillow under her head and covered her with an afghan. Then he went into the kitchen and drew a glass of water. On the counter beside the sink was the can of pepper spray that Bert had dropped on Halloween. That explained how Dalton and Travis had overpowered Lucky and locked him in the kitchen. If only they hadn't played that prank on Halloween. If only he had informed Officer Reed about the drug cache, he might have prevented the robbery and Miss Weston's brutal beating. If only...

Miss Weston took small sips of water between parched lips. Bruised skin, stretched over her skull, looked like wrinkled tissue paper with purple smudges. "I think my shoulder is broken," she said and groaned. "After they beat me, I fainted, and now I can't move my arm."

Colby looked around the room. Oil paintings were slashed and torn from the wall. A chandelier with broken crystal facets dangled from the ceiling as if someone had used it for a trapeze. Tables and chairs were overturned and upholstery ripped. Vases and mirrors were broken. Leather-bound books were scattered.

At last he heard sirens. An ambulance, followed by a police car, forced its way through the tunnel of cedars. When Dr. Perry and ambulance attendants tried to enter the house, Lucky snarled and barked so ferociously that Colby had to shut him in the kitchen again. Officer Reed and his deputy entered the room and handcuffed Dalton and Travis.

Medics carefully laid Miss Weston on a stretcher and carried her to the waiting ambulance. Colby walked by her side. Suddenly, she clutched his arm and dug her long yellow fingernails like bird claws into the flesh beneath his shirt. "Take care of Lucifer!" she commanded.

Lucifer? Lucifer? "Sure. Why, sure!" he said. Colby realized she meant Lucky.

From the verandah, he watched the ambulance roll slowly down the driveway. The cedar trees scratched its sides and slowed its progress, but at the gate, the driver turned on the siren and sped away.

Dalton and Travis staggered as they descended the verandah steps. They hung their heads and were silent as they passed Colby and climbed inside the police car. Reed turned to his deputy and said, "Get that kid's name and address, Franklin. He sure looks familiar. I'll have several questions for him, later. His 911 call probably saved Miss Weston's life. As soon as I book these two, I'll come back and we'll lock up the house."

Reed paused before he climbed into the squad car. "Hey, kid, can we count on you to take care of that dog? You're the only one who seems to have control of him. He tried to bite me. I could shoot him with a tranquilizer gun and take him to the animal shelter, but it's closed today. It's Christmas, remember?

"Yes, sir, I will. I promised Miss Weston I'd look after him."

Then Colby faced the deputy. Until that moment, he had not recognized Franklin Imotichey in his uniform. His long hair was slicked back under a brown felt Stetson, and dark glasses shadowed his eyes. Nodding curtly to Colby, as if he had never seen him before, Franklin said, "Name and address, please." Colby knew his Philip Pirrup alias would not work this time, so he gave his real name and address.

Franklin then asked, "What were you doing on the Weston premises, Colby?"

"I just had a hunch that something was wrong."

"Just a hunch, eh?" Franklin cleared his throat and tapped his pen against a notebook. "For my report, briefly describe what happened before you called 911. Then you can take the dog and go home. You look like you're ready to drop."

Colby's knees felt like rubber. He wanted to vanish, but he recounted events that led to Dalton and Travis's arrest: how he'd spotted the black Corvette in the driveway, called 911 on his mobile phone, sneaked into the house, let Lucky loose, fought Travis, untied Miss Weston, and waited for help to arrive.

While Franklin filled out his report on the verandah, Colby reentered the mansion and released Lucky from the kitchen. He wondered if he'd be arrested when Reed returned. After all, his presence at the scene in response to a mere "hunch" was not exactly the whole truth. He petted the nervous dog and spoke soothing words as he tied a leash made from a drapery cord on his collar. As they walked down the verandah steps, Franklin removed his colored glasses and smiled. "Officer Reed will contact you soon, Colby. Until then, take care of yourself, kid."

Together Colby and Lucky exited through the wrought iron gate, walked down the brick-paved lane, past the now-empty pack rat's nest, and on to Colby's house.

As he stepped through the door and into the living room, Jeanie cried, "Colby! Oh, merciful heavens! What's happened? Where did you get that dog? Have you been in an accident? Just look at those bruises! And your clothes – all torn and bloody!"

As she started toward him, Lucky growled. "Sit, Lucky," Colby said to the nervous dog. "Don't come any closer, Mom. He's just been through a bad experience, and he might bite. I'll shut him up in my room until he calms down."

"You can't keep an animal like that in the house," said Tom. "Where did you get him?"

"It's just for tonight, Dad. He's a sort of Christmas present. Tomorrow, I'll take him back to his home on Weston Hill, where he can run free."

Colby's parents' faces looked as if they were carved in stone. "I'll tell you all about it right after I take a shower and change clothes. Meantime, Mom, how about fixing a snack for Lucky and me? We're hungry!"

CHAPTER EIGHTEEN

After emergency surgery on Miss Weston's shoulder, Dr. Perry admitted her to the intensive care unit. During Christmas break, Colby checked on her progress every evening after he threw his papers and fed Lucky, but the nurse at the desk would not let him enter the unit to talk with Miss Weston.

"Relatives only," the nurse on duty said. "We'll tell her you came by." A nice brush off, Colby thought.

Too soon, Christmas vacation was over. As Colby sat in algebra class, the intercom blared, "Colby Elliott, report to the office, please."

Mary Kennedy nudged him and said, "You're in for it now, Colby." The rest of the class snickered. It was probably true. Colby's grades had hit the skids, and although a new semester was in session, he couldn't seem to concentrate.

His mind raced as he walked down the hall. Miss Weston was in the intensive care unit at the hospital, his dad was no better, and the marijuana packet was still hidden in the toe of his boot. He kept waiting for a summons from Officer Reed to explain his involvement in the attack on Miss Weston, but so far, nothing had happened.

Colby imagined the scenario. Reed will wonder why I was at Weston mansion, and then he'll remember the incident at school when the drug dog sniffed my jacket. I'll have to tell him that I've known about that stash of pot for over two months. He'll never believe that I didn't intend to smoke it or sell it. "A likely story," he'll say, when I tell him I had the drug cache under surveillance. He'll probably think I was in cahoots with Dalton and Travis.

Principal Pembroke's secretary showed him into the office. To Colby's surprise, there sat his father in a wheelchair with Dr. Perry and a man they introduced as Judge Evans.

"What's wrong, Dad?" asked Colby.

"These men need your help, son. That is, if you are willing."

Dr. Perry placed his hand on Colby's shoulder and said, "In spite of your heroic effort to save Miss Weston and get her to the hospital, Colby, she has developed pneumonia. This is not an uncommon complication in one so old and weak. She took quite a beating before you arrived. We've given her tender, loving care and medicine, but we don't expect her to live much longer. She keeps asking for you and someone named Lucifer. You and this Lucifer seem to be the only people she trusts. Judge Evans needs to know who Lucifer is, so he can notify any living relatives."

Colby smiled. "Well, sir, Lucifer is her dog. I just call him Lucky."

"A dog?" said the judge. "Are you sure? Oh, my. This is highly irregular."

"Come to the hospital with us, Colby," said Dr. Perry. "Miss Weston wants to speak with you."

Colby had been in the hospital many times after Tom's accident, but this time it was different. Under an oxygen tent, Miss Weston lay propped up on pillows. Wispy gray hair framed her face. Gasping for breath and speaking with difficulty, she said, "Come closer, boy," and with arms and hands that looked and felt like dry sticks, she reached for Colby. He moved closer to her bedside.

"Are you taking care of Lucifer?" she whispered.

"Yes, ma'am."

"Good. When he was just a pup, somebody left him to starve and die at my gate. I took him in, and since then, he's been my companion and protector. Before I die, boy, swear to me that you'll take care of him."

"I swear, Miss Weston. Lucky and I are best friends. Since you've been in the hospital, I've been feeding him every day, and we've been going rabbit hunting on your hill. But you need to get well and come home soon. Lucky misses you a lot."

A tiny smile crossed Miss Weston's face. Turning toward Judge Evans, she said, "I trust this boy, and Lucifer trusts him, too. He's the only person in fifty years that has shown me any kindness. Unknown to him, I've watched him harvesting pecans on the road and playing fetch with my dog. He's not like those other boys – the ones who planted those weeds – the ones who drove that black car and beat me because I wouldn't give them any money." She closed her eyes and sighed. "Lucifer tried to protect me, but those thugs sprayed something in his eyes."

Miss Weston coughed, and when she inhaled, her chest rattled. "This happened to me once before – back in 1930 during the flu epidemic. Papa and Sister died of pneumonia. Our servants stole Papa's gold watch, and money and jewelry from the safe and left us to die. Nobody in Bartlett cared about us. Nobody cared."

People standing around the old woman's bed looked down at the floor. They remembered the scandal and gossip and lies people had told about Miss Weston. They had believed those lies for many years and had done nothing to help the lonely old woman.

Now in a barely audible voice, Miss Weston said, "See to my will, Judge. Write it down now so that I can sign it before I die." She pointed a skeletal finger at Colby. "After you settle up my bills, this boy gets Lucifer, my house, my money, my stocks and bonds, my royalties, Weston Hill, everything." The effort of speaking with such fervor exhausted Miss Weston. She lay back on the pillow and closed her eyes.

Colby tried to tell the adults in the room about the pack rat's nest, but they motioned him to be silent. Judge Evans hastily wrote out Miss Weston's will, and she signed her name, Amanda Eucebia Weston. Dr. Perry and a nurse witnessed it.

Colby stood beside Miss Weston and held her thin, yellow hand in his warm brown one. It felt as light and dry as a dead leaf. Suddenly she sighed. Dr. Perry looked at the heart monitor and felt for her pulse. Then he listened to her heart with his stethoscope. "She's gone," he said, and he pulled the white sheet over her face.

Unable to speak without crying, Colby walked with Dr. Perry down the hall toward a reception room, where his parents were waiting. Dr. Perry said, "Miss Weston was very old, Colby, but we did everything we could to save her. So did you."

When they entered the waiting room, he expected to tell his anxious parents what had happened. Instead, Dr. Perry took one look at Tom's agonized face and postponed any conversation. Events of the day had stressed Tom physically and emotionally, and he was near a collapse.

"My God, Tom!" said Dr. Perry. "I had no idea you were in this condition. I'm admitting you to the hospital immediately."

CHAPTER NINETEEN

Colby walked out of the hospital doors into late afternoon sunshine. Dr. Perry had given Tom a sedative, and Jeanie was sitting at his bedside. If scheduled X-rays and tests developed as Dr. Perry thought they would, Tom would soon undergo surgery.

Colby had many things to do: throw his paper route, go by the house and pack a bag for his parents, feed Lucky, check with the funeral home. The funeral director couldn't understand why a teenager was in charge of making arrangements for Miss Weston's cremation and burial in the family plot on Weston Hill until Judge Evans intervened and set him straight.

Lost in thought, Colby stopped abruptly on the sidewalk. Officer Reed blocked his way and opened the back door of his patrol car. Reed grinned and said, "I think you and I have some things to discuss down at the station, Colby Elliott, alias Philip Pirrup."

Without protest, Colby climbed into the back seat. A metal grille separated prisoners from the driver in front. Just like it'll be in jail, he thought.

"How's Miss Weston doing, Colby?" Reed said.

"She didn't make it, sir."

"Oh, that's too bad. She took quite a beating."

"Yes, sir." Colby remembered from a movie he'd seen once that he shouldn't talk to a cop without a lawyer being present, but all he really wanted to do was tell Officer Reed the truth, the whole truth, and nothing but the truth from start to finish. But would Reed believe him?

They pulled up to the station. As he climbed out of the patrol car, Colby expected to be handcuffed, but Officer Reed motioned him toward the entrance and followed him inside.

The station smelled and looked just the way he remembered it. Trustees in orange coveralls were serving supper. The smell, mixed with pine-scented floor cleaner, urine, and cigarettes made him feel as if he'd eaten a live armadillo, when in fact, he hadn't eaten all day. Phones were ringing, and people were talking and shouting. He dreaded being shut up in one of those cells, even overnight. He wished he had followed Bert's advice and turned in the marijuana cache the day he discovered it.

Officer Reed opened the door to his office and motioned Colby inside. Seated in chairs or standing around the room were Mr. Pickens, Bert and Eddie and Franklin, Julie Perry, and Melissa. Everyone began talking at once.

Officer Reed said, "Whoa now. May I have your attention, please? We have some important business to discuss." He smiled. "Since your mom and dad can't be here, Lawyer Perry has agreed to represent you, Colby, We wouldn't want to violate your rights as a minor."

"Please, sir, there's no need to interrogate me. I confess. If I had told you about that cache of marijuana when I found it, Miss Weston might still be alive." Colby's voice broke. He hung his head and in a low voice said, "It's my fault that Miss Weston got hurt."

"Well, you sure took a big chance not telling us about it sooner, Colby, but Miss Weston certainly didn't blame you for what happened to her. She could have reported those men last summer after she saw Barrett and Turner harvesting marijuana in her pecan orchard."

Reed walked around his desk and picked up a folder. "Mr. Pickens suspected what was going on, Colby, so he and his nephew Eddie Imotichey were keeping the Weston Hill drug cache under surveillance, even before you discovered it. We were waiting to bust them during a drug deal." He pointed a finger at Colby. "Unfortunately, you got in the way of our investigation. Be glad that your friend Bert told his dad about your discovery of the pack rat's nest."

Colby stepped forward and said, "I took one packet of marijuana to show you what I'd found. It's still in the toe of my boot at home. I'll turn it in. Honest I will. I just kept it as evidence. I didn't sell it or smoke it or anything."

"You and Miss Weston both made mistakes by not trusting local law enforcement." Reed sat down behind his desk. "After Barrett and Turner were apprehended, Eddie suggested that bags of marijuana and other drug paraphernalia might be hidden in the trunk of Barrett's Corvette. So we got a search warrant, and Franklin opened the trunk. He found what's left of that cache of marijuana and also ingredients and equipment for making methamphetamine, a dangerous, addictive drug. We impounded the car and charged Barrett and Turner with drug possession, intent to distribute, trespassing, vandalism, assault and battery, and now, murder. They are locked up, awaiting arraignment and trial."

Reed cleared a space on his desk and motioned for Julie Perry and Franklin to come forward. "Now, what I want you to do, Colby, is give your deposition to my deputy in the presence of Lawyer Perry. These other folks have already told us what they know, so they can leave."

Eddie shook hands with Colby, and Bert and Mr. Pickens hugged him before they left the room. Colby was grateful for their friendship and regretted that he hadn't followed their good advice. Melissa gave him a warm hug and invited him for supper after he finished at the police station. "Steve will be there, and he can give you an up-to-date report on your dad."

Franklin sat at a computer and Julie Perry sat beside Colby as he told the story from start to finish about the slashed bicycle tires, the roach clip, finding the marijuana cache, making friends with Lucky, his attempt to catch the drug dealers, and Dalton and Travis's attack on Miss Weston.

When Colby and Julie emerged from the police station, a crowd of people stood at the foot of the steps. Skeeter gave him a high five and said, "Way to go, bro!" Classmates and church friends cheered. Mr. Pembroke, Mrs. McPherson and Coach Blevins smiled and shook his hand.

Linda stood at the edge of the crowd beside Mr. Jenkins. Her eyes begged Colby's forgiveness. He wondered how much she knew about Dalton's involvement in illegal drugs. To Colby, the expression, "Friends Forever," meant just that. He'd always be Linda's friend. They'd both made mistakes.

Flash bulbs popped as Mr. Kennedy snapped Colby's picture. "Wait a story!" he said. "How about an exclusive interview for the *Bartlett Banner*?"

Mary threw her arms around Colby's neck and exclaimed, "You're a hero, Cole! I'm so proud of you." He blushed, but he hugged Mary back.

At the Perry's house, Melissa had indeed prepared a feast. After supper, while she and Steve cleared the table and loaded the dishwasher, Colby told his story to Mr. Kennedy and Mary. Julie made comments about certain details in the case that should remain confidential and unpublished until after Dalton Barrett and Travis Turner were tried so that prospective jurors would not be prejudiced.

While Colby's friends discussed the secret of the pack rat's nest, he suddenly remembered that Lucky, hungry and lonesome, was waiting for him on Weston Hill. He asked Mr. Kennedy to drop him off at the school so he could get his bicycle.

As he pedaled slowly toward Weston Hill, he thought about his dad's surgery and how his recovery might affect the Elliott family. He wondered if they would move to Miss Weston's mansion. After all, Colby now owned the Weston Estate. He wondered whether Tom would recover his health and someday build patio homes on Weston Hill. He wondered if he could make the football team during spring practice.

Although it was dark, Lucky awaited his new master at the front gate. He barked a greeting and placed his paws on Colby's chest. His long red tongue swiped across Colby's face, and his tail swished back and forth.

"Glad to see me, aren't you, boy?" Colby rubbed the dog's head and muzzle and patted his sleek sides. Then the two raced up the lane through the cedars toward Weston mansion.

Martha Rhynes, a retired teacher, began her writing career by researching the lives of American authors and writing biographies and analyses of their work for inclusion in literary encyclopedias. Her book-length biographies include, *I, Too, Sing America, The Story of Langston Hughes*; *Gwendolyn Brooks, Poet from Chicago*; *Ralph Ellison: Author of Invisible Man*; *Jack London: Writer of Adventure*; and *Ray Bradbury: A Teller of Tales*. Her works of fiction include numerous short stories and three novels: *The Secret of the Pack Rat's Nest*; *The War Bride*; and *Man on First*. Rhynes is the mother of six adult children and many grandchildren. Her family operates a cattle ranch in Oklahoma.

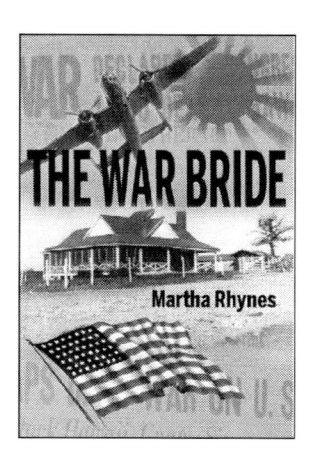

THE WAR BRIDE
by Martha E. Rhynes

    Milly and Robert fall in love on December 7, 1941, the same day the Japanese attack Pearl Harbor. He becomes a Marine pilot, and they marry. While war rages on two continents, she awaits his return from the South Pacific. Raised in Tulsa, Milly moves to Robert's isolated ranch and becomes Uncle Charley's cook and ranch hand. Together, they survive dangerous weather and tragedy involving neighbors at Eureka Springs.
    Meanwhile, Robert flies bombing missions over an enemy supply base and transports men and supplies to the island from which the atomic bomb is launched. Letters keep Milly and Robert's marriage alive during the war, but both have changed during their long wartime separation. Will their love survive until Robert finally comes home?

ENJOY UNFORGETTABLE CHARACTERS AND AUTHENTIC HISTORICAL DETAILS IN THIS ROMANTIC NOVEL.

ON SALE NOW AT AMAZON, BARNES & NOBLE, OTHER ONLINE RETAILERS & SELECT BOOKSTORES!

ISBN 978-1432759353

JACK LONDON: WRITER OF ADVENTURE
by Martha E. Rhynes

Jack London not only wrote about adventure, he lived it. During his lifetime, he was the most popular and prolific writer in America. Readers idolized him. They loved his action-packed stories with their vivid descriptions and psychological insights into human and animal behavior. They didn't know he had lived these stories in real-life adventures on American's frontier.

From Klondike gold rush stories to wild sea adventures, he experienced life as many of his characters would. And he also wrote articles and books dealing with prison reform, alcoholism, and radical economic and social theories. A war correspondent during the Russo-Japanese War, London sought excitement at every turn. His famous novels include *The Call of the Wild, The Sea Wolf, White Fang, Martin Eden,* and *The Iron Heel.*

London lived an amazing life and left an amazing literary legacy for readers to enjoy – golden nuggets between the covers of his books.

ENJOY JACK LONDON'S THRILLING ADVENTURES!

ON SALE NOW AT AMAZON, BARNES & NOBLE, OTHER ONLINE RETAILERS & SELECT BOOKSTORES!

ISBN 978-1432772826